W9-ACD-990

WITHDRAWN

HERMAN MELVILLE was born in 1819 in New York City. After his father's death he left school for a series of clerical jobs before going to sea as a young man of nineteen. At twenty-one he shipped aboard the whaler *Acushnet* and began a series of adventures in the South Seas that would last for three years and form the basis for his first two novels, *Typee* and *Omoo.* Although these two novels sold well and gained for Melville a measure of fame, nineteenth-century readers were puzzled by the experiments with form that he began with his third novel, *Mardi,* and continued brilliantly in his masterpiece, *Moby-Dick.* During his later years spent working as a customs inspector on the New York docks, Melville published only poems, compiled in a collection entitled *Battle-Pieces,* and died in 1891 with *Billy Budd, Sailor,* now considered a classic, still unpublished.

This Enriched Classics edition of Herman Melville's *Billy Budd, Sailor* is introduced by Cyrus R. K. Patell, Assistant Professor of English at New York University, where he teaches nineteenth- and twentieth-century American literature. He is associate editor of *The Cambridge History of American Literature, Volume One: 1590–1820* and *Volume Two: Prose Writing, 1820–1865.* He is currently completing a study of twentieth-century American fiction and the problem of Emersonian individualism.

**Titles available in the
ENRICHED CLASSICS SERIES**

Herman Melville

Billy Budd, Sailor

Introduced by
Cyrus R. K. Patell

WASHINGTON SQUARE PRESS
PUBLISHED BY POCKET BOOKS

New York London Toronto Sydney Tokyo Singapore

This book is a work of fiction. Names, characters, places and incidents are products of the author's imagination or are used fictitiously. Any resemblance to actual events or locales or persons, living or dead, is entirely coincidental.

A Washington Square Press Publication of
POCKET BOOKS, a division of Simon & Schuster Inc.
1230 Avenue of the Americas, New York, NY 10020

Introduction, critical excerpts, and supplementary materials copyright © 1999 by Simon & Schuster Inc.

ISBN: 0-671-02833-2

First Washington Square Press printing March 1999

10 9 8 7 6 5 4 3 2 1

WASHINGTON SQUARE PRESS and colophon are registered trademarks of Simon & Schuster Inc.

Photo research and captions by Cheryl Moch

Cover art by Dan Craig

Printed in the U.S.A.

Contents

Introduction

In December 1885, Herman Melville finally retired from his job at the New York Custom House. Unable to support himself through his writing, he had been working there for nineteen years as a customs inspector. He was sixty-six years old, and he had not written fiction in almost thirty years, though he had been writing and publishing poetry steadily. At some point during the following two years, he began to work on a poem that would eventually be called "Billy in the Darbies," about a mutinous sailor, shackled aboard ship, awaiting his execution. The poem was intended for inclusion in a volume of poetry to be called *John Marr and Other Sailors* (1888), and Melville wrote a prose headnote to accompany it. Then the story began to grow and change in Melville's imagination, and he returned to it, expanding the headnote into a novella that he would revise throughout the remaining years of his life.

At the time of Melville's death in 1891, the manuscript of the novella was sequentially complete, but Melville was still revising its language and thematic emphases. In addition, the manuscript itself was found in a condition of such physical disarray that the presentation of an authoritative version became difficult, if not impossible. The novella was finally published in 1924, its text edited by Raymond Weaver and given the title *Billy Budd, Foretopman*; a subsequent edition was produced for Harvard University Press by F. Barron Freeman in 1948. Critical dissatisfaction with the choices made by both of these editors led to the production of a new "reading text" by Harrison Hayford and Merton M. Sealts, Jr. in 1962, which they presented with a lengthy commentary explaining their editorial decisions and a "genetic text," a literal transcription of the surviving leaves of Melville's manuscript. In addition, Hayford and Sealts changed the title of the novella from *Billy Budd, Foretopman* to *Billy Budd, Sailor (An Inside Narrative),* which appears on the first page of Melville's manuscript. The Hayford-Sealts text is the one that we have used for this Washington Square Press edition.

Why had the author of *Moby-Dick* (1851) stopped writing fiction for so long? When *Moby-Dick* was published, Melville was quite well known as a writer of sea tales. He had already published *Typee* (1846) and *Omoo* (1847), two semiautobiographical novels based on his experiences a decade earlier as a sailor in the South Seas. Melville's third novel, *Mardi* (1849), was less popular than its predecessors because of its radical experimentation with narrative style, and Melville returned briefly to more conventional forms of narrative: in the year before he began to write *Moby-Dick,* Melville published two novels, *Redburn* (1849) and *White-Jacket* (1850), which he described as "two jobs, which I have done for money—being forced to it, as other men are to sawing wood." By the spring of 1850, Melville had become a father, and that summer, full of confidence in his new writing project—the "whaling voyage"—Melville moved his family to Pittsfield, Massachusetts, where he bought a farm that he named Arrowhead. By mid-1850, Melville's family life had stabilized, and his prospects looked good. That June, Melville offered his "new work" to the English publisher Richard Bentley, promising it for "the coming autumn" and describing it as "a romance of adventure, founded upon certain wild legends in the Southern Sperm whale Fisheries, and illustrated by the author's own personal experience, of two years & more, as a harpooneer." A book, in other words, very much like his early successes *Typee* and *Omoo.*

Moby-Dick, however, turned out to be something else altogether, in large part because in the middle of writing it, Melville befriended Nathaniel Hawthorne. The meeting took place on August 5, 1850, at a picnic near Pittsfield, and it inspired Melville not only to go back and read Hawthorne's *Mosses from an Old Manse* (1846), but also to dash off the now-famous two-part essay, "Hawthorne and His Mosses." The first part was published in *Literary World* a mere twelve days after his meeting with Hawthorne. In the essay, Melville compares Hawthorne to Shakespeare, describing them both as "masters of the great Art of Telling the Truth." Although he acknowledges that some of his readers may be surprised "to read on Shakespeare and Hawthorne on the same page," he refuses to pull any punches and makes the daring assertion that "Shakespeare has been approached. There are minds that have gone as far as Shakespeare into the universe." Moreover, "if Shakespeare has not been equalled, give the world time, and he is sure to be surpassed, in one hemisphere or the other." Melville even seemed to be placing his bets on *this* hemisphere: like Emerson's famous oration "The American Scholar" (1837) and the famous "Preface to *Leaves of Grass*" that Walt Whitman would write in 1855, "Hawthorne and His Mosses" is an American literary manifesto, a call for American writers to take up the challenge of equaling and perhaps even surpassing Shakespeare. It is a call that Melville himself seemed to be answering when he returned to the manuscript of *Moby-Dick* a few days later.

When it was published, *Moby-Dick*'s encyclopedic scope and experiments in narrative technique puzzled readers and critics alike. Reviews were decidedly mixed, and sales were disappointing. Dissatisfied by the response of readers and critics to his magnum opus and embittered by what he perceived as shabby treatment from his publisher, Melville wrote the enigmatic novel *Pierre,* which contained a bitter indictment of American readers and publishers. It was a commercial failure and left his career, so full of promise a few years earlier, in a shambles. Melville would go on to publish the novel *Israel Potter* (1855), *The Piazza Tales* (which contained the now-famous stories "Bartleby the Scrivener" and "Benito Cereno"), and *The Confidence-Man* (1857) before turning to poetry, giving up fiction and with it all hope of earning a living as a writer. His first volume of verse, *Battle-Pieces and Aspects of the War* (1866), was published privately. Four months after it appeared, Melville received an appointment as a customs inspector on the New York docks,

which gave him a steady income. Although he continued
to write during evenings, weekends and vacations, his later
life was marred by ill health, the suicide of his eldest son,
and the premature death of his second son. Melville died
in obscurity without a single obituary to mark his passing,
but in 1919 a celebration of the centennial of his birth
initiated an important reevaluation of his work. The
publication of *Billy Budd* in 1924 bolstered Melville's
reputation and would help to secure for him the preemi-
nent place in American literary history that he now
enjoys.

In *Billy Budd*, Melville returns to the questions of fate,
divinity, and humankind's place in the universe that
haunted him in *Moby-Dick*. One of the most famous
chapters in *Moby-Dick* is a self-contained tale called
"The Town-Ho's Story," in which a shipboard conflict
between a sailor and a first mate is resolved when the first
mate is killed by the white whale Moby Dick, in what
appears to be a divine judgment. A similar act of seemingly divine judgment lies at the heart of *Billy Budd*,
which explores what happens when two systems of
justice—the human and the divine—prove to be incompatible with one another. Billy, the "Handsome Sailor"
who is respected and even adored by his shipmates, is
unjustly accused of plotting mutiny by the ship's master-
at-arms, John Claggart, whose action seems motivated
only by an inexplicable inborn malice. Literally shocked
into speechlessness when accused by Claggart in the
presence of Captain Vere, Billy strikes out at the master-
at-arms with his fist. The blow, which seems to occur as if
by reflex rather than by premeditated intent, proves fatal.
Vere, calling Billy the "fated boy," believes in his heart
that Billy has played the role of God's avenging angel, but
he also realizes that Billy's action has made him a
criminal under military law. "Struck dead by an angel of
God!" he exclaims. "Yet the angel must hang." Sentenced
to die by a hastily convened "drumhead" military court,
Billy forgives his executioners: his final words are "God
bless Captain Vere!"

According to Harrison Hayford and Merton M. Sealts,
Jr., the editors of the authoritative 1962 text of the

novella, Melville first imagined Billy as "an older man, condemned for fomenting mutiny and apparently guilty as charged." But Melville deepened his conception of his protagonist as he went along, and by November 1888 he had completed a manuscript of more than 150 pages, in which Billy had become the "upright barbarian" sentenced to hang for killing John Claggart, the master-at-arms who had accused him falsely. This new direction seems to have been precipitated at least in part by the appearance of a magazine article the previous June about the mutiny aboard the U.S. brig-of-war *Somers* in 1842. During a peacetime training cruise, three crewmen aboard the *Somers* were peremptorily hanged for conspiracy to mutiny by Captain Alexander Slidell Mackenzie, without the benefit of being formally arraigned, tried, allowed to confront witnesses or offer any defense. One of the executed men was Philip Spencer, an acting midshipman who was the son of the secretary of war. Melville's cousin Guert Gansevoort was a first lieutenant aboard the *Somers* and was one of the officers whom Mackenzie consulted before reaching his verdict. Although Mackenzie was formally vindicated afterward, his handling of the incident never ceased to be controversial, and Guert Gansevoort remained haunted by his part in it for the rest of his life. The appearance of the 1888 article and of a three-part article entitled "The Murder of Philip Spencer" the following year in *Cosmopolitan* seems to have provoked Melville to take up once again the questions of justice, authority, and fate that animated his great novel *Moby-Dick* nearly forty years earlier.

In the last three years of his life, Melville was continually revising the manuscript of *Billy Budd*, which grew to a final length of 351 pages and was left in the form of a semifinal draft at his death in 1891. The third and last phase of Melville's revisions involved fleshing out the character of the ship's captain, Edward Fairfax Vere, who had been simply a witness to the confrontation between Billy and Claggart in the earlier versions. Indeed, Vere's role was so minor in the second version that only a few manuscript pages stood between Claggart's death and the introduction of the ballad that concludes the story. It was during this late period of revision that Melville added the sections of the novella that have fascinated and haunted its readers: the chapters devoted to the analysis of Vere's character, Billy's trial, Vere's extended address to the court, and Billy's execution. In fact, Vere's role in the final manuscript is so enlarged that many readers have felt that it is Captain Vere, rather than Billy Budd, who is the novella's true protagonist.

Billy Budd dramatizes the inscrutability of human motivation. The triangular conflict that Melville creates raises a set of questions for which there may be no definitive or satisfactory answers. What is Claggart's motivation in accusing Billy Budd? Why does Vere rush to bring Billy to judgment? Is Billy guilty or innocent? To help us begin to answer these questions, Melville offers us four different frames of reference: the historical, the mythological, the biblical, and the sexual. The British novelist E. M. Forster once wrote that the story of *Billy Budd* "has the quality of a Greek myth: it is so basic and so fertile that it can be retold or dramatized in various ways." Forster might have been be right about Melville's *story,* but what makes Melville's *novella* a literary masterpiece is the *particular* way in which it tells this story, for what Melville has done in *Billy Budd* is to tell this "basic" story in four different ways—simultaneously.

Billy Budd is, first of all, a historical story with political overtones. It is set not in Melville's day but "in the summer of 1797," during the Napoleonic Wars, a time when Britain was at war with France. The political overtones are apparent from the first page of the novella, when Melville chooses to illustrate the concept of the "Handsome Sailor" by describing "a common sailor so intensely black that he must needs have been a native African of the unadulterate blood of Ham." Melville is alluding to the story of Noah's grandson, Ham, who is cursed by his grandfather with the words "a slave of slaves shall he be to his brothers." What Melville is suggesting here is that contrary to what his readers might believe, those who possess the "blood of Ham" can also possess a seemingly natural nobility of character. Melville also includes a reference to Jean-Baptiste du Val de Grâce, Baron de

Cloots, a Prussian-born revolutionary who introduced a multiracial assortment of men before the French National Assembly as a show of support for the French Revolution. Together, these two allusions serve as an indictment of cultures—including Melville's own—that discriminate against those who are nonwhite. Melville used a reference to Cloots in *Moby-Dick* for similar purposes; in that book, he also described the nobility of the "pagan" harpooner Queequeg by comparing him to George Washington. We see immediately that, like *Moby-Dick,* the novella *Billy Budd* begins by championing an idea of interracial brotherhood that in Melville's day was politically quite progressive.

What the novella dramatizes, however, is that human ideals such as brotherhood are readily sacrificed to the necessities of politics. In 1797, the British fleet patrolling the North Sea was constantly on alert and ready to engage in hostilities with the French navy and its Spanish and Dutch allies. But tensions were particularly high at the moment that Melville is describing because of an event known as "the Great Mutiny," which was actually the second of two insurrections within the British navy that spring. The first mutiny occurred at Spithead, a "roadstead" or protected anchorage in the English Channel between Portsmouth and the Isle of Wight, on April 15. It was fueled by the grievances of sailors who were badly fed, seldom paid, and brutally punished to maintain discipline. Moreover, many of these sailors had been forced into the navy through impressment, a common way of "recruiting" sailors for the English navy during the Napoleonic Wars. Impressment was essentially the practice of drafting seamen into the navy by any means necessary. In the third chapter of *Billy Budd* we see young Billy taken from his merchant ship, called the *Rights-of-Man,* and pressed into service upon the warship *Bellipotent.* Melville has chosen his names carefully. The name *Rights-of-Man* comes from Thomas Paine's tract *The Rights of Man* (1791), written in response to Edmund Burke's conservative *Reflections on the Revolution in France* (1790). Burke's book argued for the priority of social institutions; Paine's, for the priority of natural rights. In moving from the *Rights-of-Man* to the *Bellipotent* (Latin for "powerful in war"), Billy is entering into the authoritarian and repressive world of martial law, where natural rights are severely curtailed and subordinated to military discipline.

The Spithead mutiny ended when British naval authorities granted the sailors' claims, Parliament voted to raise their pay, and the mutinous sailors received a royal pardon. On May 12, however, a more serious outbreak of mutiny occurred in the North Sea fleet, which was blockading the Dutch coast. Mutineers seized the ships and sailed back to the Nore, a sandbank at the mouth of the Thames. The mutiny lasted for a month, and once the sailors had returned to their duties, the ringleader and eighteen others were hanged. These two mutinies form a crucial historical context for the action of *Billy Budd:* they influence Captain Vere's decision to act quickly and to follow what he believes to be the letter of military law, in order to maintain strict military discipline and avert the chance of mutiny.

Melville, however, suggests another historical context within which to judge Vere's actions, one that requires us to look forward rather than backward. For at the end of his description of the Nore Mutiny, Melville tells us that among the "thousands of mutineers were some of the tars who not so very long afterwards . . . helped to win a coronet for Nelson at the Nile, and the naval crown of crowns for him at Trafalgar." The year after the Nore Mutiny (and the action of *Billy Budd*), Rear Admiral Sir Horatio Nelson would lead the British fleet to victory in the Battle of the Nile, receiving a baron's coronet as a reward. Seven years later, at the decisive Battle of Trafalgar, his fleet would destroy twenty French and Spanish ships while losing none of its own, but Nelson would be mortally wounded. In death, he would achieve lasting renown—the "naval crown of crowns." Melville interrupts the flow of his narrative by devoting an entire chapter to a discussion of Nelson's career, and we realize that he is setting up Nelson as a model against which to measure the captain of the *Bellipotent*. Captain Vere is a poor man's Nelson. In chapter 7, we learn that Vere is a man of learning who prizes "books treating of actual men and events no matter of what era—history, biography, and unconventional writers like Montaigne, who free from cant and convention, honestly and in the spirit of common sense philosophize upon realities." Vere's reading marks him as an "exceptional character," and we are also told that he is Nelson's equal as a "seaman or fighter." Moreover, like Nelson, Vere will die in action at sea, though tellingly it will be before Nelson's great victories at the Nile and Trafalgar.

Melville suggests that what makes Vere a lesser man than Nelson is the fact that he lacks Nelson's vision and his magnanimity of spirit. Melville's use of Nelson as a historical frame of reference shows us that Vere is short-sighted. He does not realize that the Nore Mutiny was simply "the distempering irruption of contagious fever in a frame constitutionally sound," a serious but not a fatal illness. In rushing to judge Billy, Vere is acting as if only the most drastic remedy could cure the navy's ills: to save the body, he amputates a limb. There is "a queer streak of the pedantic" within Vere, whereas Nelson was the kind of individual who inspired poets. Indeed, for Melville, the poet's lines fail to do justice to Nelson's deeds: "the poet but embodies in verse those exaltations of sentiment that a nature like Nelson, the opportunity being given, vitalizes into acts." It is his "queer streak of the pedantic" that will lead Vere to act according to the dictates of a court that he knows to be "arbitrary" and unmerciful—the military court—even though he is convinced that on the day of the Last Judgment, Billy Budd will be acquitted of wrongdoing. Melville's descriptions of Nelson cause us to suspect that Nelson, had he been in Vere's position, would have found a way to be less arbitrary and more merciful. Indeed, Melville tells us that in the same year the events of *Billy Budd* are taking place, Nelson managed to quell the threat of mutiny aboard the ship *Theseus*: his method was not to "terrorize the crew into base subjection, but to win them, by force of his mere presence and heroic personality, back to an allegiance if not as enthusiastic as his own yet as true." In short, the historical setting that Melville evokes renders Vere's action explicable but not venerable.

Vere is a man who cannot transcend his moment, unlike Admiral Nelson—and unlike Billy Budd.

The reference to the story of Ham that appears on the first page of the novella does more than simply indicate the presence of a political subtext to the novella. It also suggests to us that as we read *Billy Budd,* the Bible will prove to be a crucial *intertext,* a text that completes the meaning of a literary work. Biblical references abound in *Billy Budd,* and they constitute an invitation to read the novella as a Christian allegory akin to John Bunyan's *Pilgrim's Progress.* Melville stresses Billy's seemingly natural innocence early on, suggesting that he seems to belong "to a period prior to Cain's city and citified man." In Genesis 4, we learn that Adam's son Cain, having killed his brother Abel, is banished from the face of God and forced to leave the countryside; he eventually founds a city in the land of Nod. Billy appears to be a throwback to the time before the Fall, when humankind existed in a state of nature and was not acquainted with death. Many readers view Billy as an "American Adam" and his story as a latter-day version of the Fall. Billy, the innocent, is tempted by the satanic Claggart and breaks the law. For his transgression, he is punished by a heavenly father, the captain and shipmaster known as "Starry Vere," and sentenced to die, the fate to which Adam and all of his progeny are doomed after the Fall. In this reading, *Billy Budd* exists as Melville's meditation on the impermanence of human innocence, and on the fact that humanity exists in a fallen state surrounded by evil.

The story of the Fall from Grace is one of the most familiar in Western culture. If Melville invites us to read his novella as a version of the Fall, he also warns that we may not want to be so quick to accept his invitation. In chapter 11, when Melville describes the character of the master-at-arms, John Claggart, he suggests that we are too much ruled by the story of the Fall and the notion of original sin that arises as its consequence. He takes issue in particular with the Calvinist notion of the "total depravity of mankind." Calvinism, the doctrine that is based upon the writings of the French theologian John Calvin (1509–1564), rests on the belief that, after the Fall, human beings were inherently sinful and doomed to damnation. Calvinists believed, however, that as a result of Christ's sacrifice, certain men and women could be chosen by God for salvation; they would receive "grace" and go to heaven, without regard to their deeds or their manner of life. Because all human beings are by nature sinful or "depraved," none of them can be said to deserve God's grace, nor can they earn it. The chosen ones receive it simply because God is merciful. Melville chafes at this idea that all human beings are inherently depraved, and when he describes Claggart's "natural depravity," he makes it clear that he is not invoking the Calvinist conception of depravity. Claggart is not depraved because he is like all other human beings. In fact, Claggart's depravity makes him different and sets him apart. Melville's description of Claggart thus serves a double purpose: it helps Melville invoke the story of the Fall but it also allows him to question the ways in which that story has been traditionally interpreted.

The biblical flavor of Melville's novella has also led many readers to see it as a version of the Christ story. Billy is a foundling of uncertain parentage, though we are told that "noble descent was as evident in him as in a blood horse." We learn that he is a natural "peacemaker," and that he can transform a ship that is a "rat-pit of quarrels" into a harmonious community of companions. Like Christ, he is falsely accused, sentenced to death, and accepts his fate with humility. In the moments before his execution, Billy utters something quite unexpected: "God bless Captain Vere!" As he is hauled into the air by the neck, his flight is described in terms that evoke the first chapter of the Book of Revelation: "At the same moment it chanced that the vapory fleece hanging low in the East was shot through with a soft glory as of the fleece of the Lamb of God seen in mystical vision." Melville's rendering of this scene implies that we should understand *Billy Budd* as a dramatization of the power of Christian love. In his attempt to avoid mutiny by dispensing swift justice, Vere inadvertently brings his crew to the brink of mutiny by sentencing Billy Budd to death. In the end, it is Billy who saves the day by bestowing his blessing upon the captain. It is passages such as these that led the first editor of *Billy Budd*, Raymond Weaver, to describe the novella in terms that recall John Milton's *Paradise Lost*, as Melville's attempt "to justify the ways of God to man."

Other critics, however, have been less convinced that we should read *Billy Budd* solely as a Christian allegory, noting that Melville has also filled his text with a large number of references to Greek and Roman mythology. In other words, if Melville invites us to see Billy's story as a retelling of the Fall or of the story of Christ's martyrdom, he also invites us to view it as an example of classical tragedy. Early in the second chapter, Billy is compared to the hero Hercules—or, more precisely, to a statue of Hercules that a "Greek sculptor" might have crafted. The effect of the comparison is not only to indicate Billy's heroism but also to emphasize something else—his beauty—as if he were an object of art to be admired. With just this brief mythological reference, Melville foreshadows Billy's fate, and he continues this pattern at the end of chapter 9, when he compares Billy to Achilles, the powerful warrior who fought at Troy. Dipped in the River Styx by his mother, Thetis, Achilles was rendered invulnerable to pain or death, except at the heel, where she held him and where the enchanted waters therefore did not touch. Fearing for his safety, Thetis hid Achilles by disguising him as a young girl, but he was discovered by the crafty prince Odyssey and taken to war. Ultimately, Achilles was killed when a poisoned arrow from the bow of the Trojan prince Paris struck the spot left untouched by the enchanted waters. The phrase "Achilles heel" thus denotes a point of vulnerability. The comparison suggests that Billy, too, will have an "Achilles heel" that will be his undoing.

Billy's tragic flaw proves to be his inability to use words in anything but the simplest of ways. In the early chapters of the book, we learn that Billy's simple nature makes him beloved among his shipmates. He is described by his first captain as a natural "peacemaker," who exudes an aura of "virtue," but what cements Billy in his shipmates' affection is the fact that when challenged by a gruff shipmate, he strikes out with his fist and gives "the burly fool a drubbing." Billy's air of natural heroism arises from his innocence, from his inability "to deal in double meanings and insinuations of any sort." When Billy is forced to confront those who do deal in insinuations, however, he becomes paralyzed, unable to speak or use words at all. Attempting to explain why he struck Claggart dead, Billy says, "Could I have used my tongue I would not have struck him. But he foully lied to my face and in presence of my captain, and I had to say something, and I could only say it with a blow, God help me!" Billy's tragedy is that he is ill equipped to live in a world of double meanings; his forthrightness sets him apart from his fellows, but it dooms him in the end. We must also remember that we are reading his story in a text that is itself full of double meanings, allusions, puns, and all manner of literary inside jokes. The very style with which Melville has chosen to tell Billy's story demonstrates both the appeal and the inadequacy of his brand of innocent heroism.

There is, finally, one more way to understand why Billy must suffer the fate he does, and it, too, is suggested by the mythological allusions to Hercules and Achilles. For as the comparison to Hercules emphasizes Billy's natural heroism, it also calls attention to his almost feminine beauty: "The ear, small and shapely, the arch of the foot, the curve in mouth and nostril, . . . above all, something in the mobile expression, and every chance attitude and movement, something suggestive of a mother eminently favored by Love and the Graces." Billy's femininity is further insinuated by the comparison to Achilles, who was girlish enough in his youthful appearance to be hidden among women by his mother in her hopes to prevent him from going to war. Billy's nickname aboard the *Bellipotent* is Beauty, a name that we would expect to be reserved for someone who is at least potentially the object of erotic feelings.

Billy Budd, in short, is also a story about homosexuality, and about what happens when a culture teaches individuals to regard same-sex erotic feelings as evil or unnatural. Melville was writing at a time when the concept of "the homosexual" had only recently been defined. Same-sex eroticism is, of course, as old as the world, but the idea of sexual orientation, according to which same-sex erotic attraction, if present, constitutes an abiding and defining characteristic of personal identity, is relatively recent. Indeed, it is thought that the term *homosexuality* did not exist before 1869, when it appeared in a pamphlet written by Karl Maria Kertbeny entitled "An Open Letter to the Prussian Minister of Justice." Classical Greek has no word for *homosexual* because ancient Greek culture understood sexuality as a matter of preference rather than orientation, liable to change from occasion to occasion—at least as far as men were concerned. The course of scientific research into the nature of homosexuality was profoundly influenced by Richard Freiherr von Krafft-Ebing's treatise *Psychopathia Sexualis* (1886), which depicted homosexuality as a pathological condition. Krafft-Ebing devoted a hundred pages in the first edition of the treatise to a discussion of "antipathic sexual instinct"; he would adopt Kertbeny's term *homosexualität* in subsequent editions. Rejecting the contention that homosexuality was in any way "natural," he argued that the only "natural" sexuality was procreative, heterosexual sexuality.

Melville's novella depicts a character who fits the late-nineteenth-century stereotype of the homosexual, but it is not the title character: rather, it is Claggart, the master-at-arms. At his trial, Billy is asked, "Now why should [Claggart] have so lied, so maliciously lied, since you declare there was no malice between you?" Billy has no adequate answer, and Vere quickly sweeps the question aside as immaterial to the matter of Billy's guilt. One answer, of course, is that Claggart is simply the embodiment of evil, an incarnation of Satan, who simply hates Billy's completely innocent nature. However, Melville's narrator also suggests that Claggart's nature cannot be fully comprehended unless we are able to turn "to some authority not liable to the charge of being tinctured with the biblical element." Moreover, we are told that "to pass from a normal nature to [Claggart] one must cross 'the deadly space between.' And this is best done by indirection." In other words, Melville is going to try to tell us something about Claggart without saying it openly. Could this be "the love that dares not speak its name" (to quote the phrase that Oscar Wilde would use just a few years later during his trial for homosexual practices)? Claggart's antipathy toward Billy is described over and over as a "passion," and Melville's narrator surmises that what "had first moved [Claggart] against Billy" was the latter's "significant personal beauty." We learn that Claggart could sometimes be seen with a "meditative and melancholy expression, his eyes strangely suffused with incipient feverish tears." At such moments, Melville tells us, "the melancholy expression would have in it a touch of soft yearning, as if Claggart could even have loved Billy but for fate and ban." These passages suggest that Claggart suffers from an unspeakable desire that ultimately renders Billy himself speechless.

It is significant that when Melville describes Claggart's melancholy, he makes an allusion to "the Man of Sorrows" from Isaiah 53:3, a figure who was generally read as a foreshadowing of Christ. Because Billy is surrounded by so much Christ imagery, the reference here serves to suggest that Billy and Claggart are in fact doubles of one another; it also renders Claggart, however briefly, a sympathetic figure. It suggests that Claggart's "depravity" is a result of the self-hatred that the homosexual who lives in a homophobic culture is taught to feel for himself. From this standpoint, Claggart's accusation arises from the fact that Billy's beauty threatens to awaken Claggart's repressed desires and potentially those of the others on the ship. In Melville's day, as in ours, same-sex eroticism was thought to be incompatible with military discipline, and therefore Billy, through no fault of his own, poses a threat that must be stamped out. In sentencing Billy to death, Vere thus continues the work that Claggart has begun, very possibly because he, too, has barely repressed erotic feelings for the Handsome Sailor. We are told that "the Handsome Sailor as a signal figure among the crew had naturally enough attracted the captain's attention from the first." Vere thinks of Billy as "a fine specimen of the *genus homo,* who in the nude might have posed for a statue of young Adam before the Fall." The biblical reference here serves to deflect attention away from the fact that for Vere to have this thought requires him to have imagined Billy in the nude. Is it possible that Vere brushes aside the question of Claggart's motivation because he wants certain things to remain unspoken, because he wants to deflect attention away from his own feelings?

These motifs within *Billy Budd* have made it an object of interest recently for the school of literary criticism known as "queer theory," but the idea that the novella is at least in part "about" homosexuality is not new. In a well-known essay written only nine years after the initial publication of *Billy Budd*, E. L. Grant Watson suggests that "from behind—from far behind the main pageant of the story—there seem to fall suggestive shadows of primal, sexual simplicities." For Watson, Melville's portrayal of "the homosexually-disposed Claggart" is part of the psychological realism of the novella, written by an author who had already, in his earlier novel *Pierre,* "as surely as any modern psychoanalyst, discovered all the major complexes that have since received baptism at the hands of Freudians."

Billy Budd is an archetypal figure, a scapegoat who is finally sacrificed for the good of his community. But why—or for whom—must he be sacrificed? The different ways of reading the story that Melville embeds into his novella offer a number of possibilities. Ultimately, the novella suggests that Billy's fate is *overdetermined,* that it is the result not of one deciding cause but many. Melville called *Billy Budd* "an inside narrative" in order to let us know that it should be taken as an insider's account of an episode that can be depicted only inaccurately in official reports, newspapers, and seamen's anecdotes.

In the final two chapters of the novella, we are given both "an account of the affair" that appears "in a naval chronicle of the time, an authorized weekly publication" and a ballad written by one of Billy's shipmates. Neither of these versions can offer us the subtle and rich account that we have been given in the preceding twenty-eight chapters. The account that appears in the chronicle is an outsider's version of the affair, and predictably it contains distortions. The ballad, however, is an insider's account, and it shows us that simply being an insider is not enough. Melville describes the ballad as a "rude utterance," not at all literary. Melville thus implies that literary art is the result of the ability to probe past surface appearances to the inward truth that lies below, what Hawthorne described in his preface to *The House of the Seven Gables* (1851) as "the truth of the human heart." Because the ballad, "Billy in the Darbies," was actually written before the novella, Melville's decision to call attention to its limitations by reproducing it at the end of *Billy Budd* suggests that as he approached the end of his writing career, Melville rediscovered the power of prose fiction. It is as if the story of the young sailor Billy Budd was too potent to be contained within a brief ballad, as if it demanded the particular kind of subtle and detailed presentation that is possible only in prose fiction.

Cyrus R. K. Patell

Billy Budd, Sailor

(An Inside Narrative)[1]

Dedicated to JACK CHASE,[1] Englishman
Wherever that great heart may now be
Here on Earth or harbored in Paradise
Captain of the Maintop in the year 1843
in the U.S. Frigate *United States*

I

In the time before steamships, or then more frequently than now, a stroller along the docks of any considerable seaport would occasionally have his attention arrested by a group of bronzed mariners, man-of-war's men or merchant sailors in holiday attire, ashore on liberty. In certain instances they would flank, or like a bodyguard quite surround, some superior figure of their own class, moving along with them like Aldebaran[1] among the lesser lights of his constellation. That signal object was the "Handsome Sailor" of the less prosaic time alike of the military and merchant navies. With no perceptible trace of the vainglorious about him, rather with the offhand unaffectedness of natural regality, he seemed to accept the spontaneous homage of his shipmates.

A somewhat remarkable instance recurs to me. In Liverpool, now half a century ago, I saw under the shadow of the great dingy street-wall of Prince's Dock (an obstruction long since removed) a common sailor so intensely black that he must needs have been a native African of the unadulterate blood of Ham[2]—a symmetric figure much above the average height. The two ends of a gay silk handkerchief thrown loose about the neck danced upon the displayed ebony of his chest, in his ears were big hoops of gold, and a Highland bonnet with a tartan band set off his shapely head. It was a hot noon in July; and his face, lustrous with perspiration, beamed with barbaric good humor. In jovial sallies right and left, his white teeth flashing into view, he rollicked along, the center of a company of his shipmates. These were made up of such an assortment of tribes and complexions as would have well fitted them to be marched by Anacharsis Cloots[3] before the bar of the first French Assembly as Representatives of the Human Race. At each spontaneous tribute rendered by the wayfarers to this black pagod[4] of a fellow—the tribute

3

of a pause and stare, and less frequently an exclamation—the motley retinue showed that they took that sort of pride in the evoker of it which the Assyrian priests doubtless showed for their grand sculptured Bull when the faithful prostrated themselves.

To return. If in some cases a bit of a nautical Murat[5] in setting forth his person ashore, the Handsome Sailor of the period in question evinced nothing of the dandified Billy-be-Dam, an amusing character all but extinct now, but occasionally to be encountered, and in a form yet more amusing than the original, at the tiller of the boats on the tempestuous Erie Canal[6] or, more likely, vaporing in the groggeries along the towpath. Invariably a proficient in his perilous calling, he was also more or less of a mighty boxer or wrestler. It was strength and beauty. Tales of his prowess were recited. Ashore he was the champion; afloat the spokesman; on every suitable occasion always foremost. Close-reefing topsails in a gale, there he was, astride the weather yardarm-end, foot in the Flemish horse as stirrup, both hands tugging at the earing as at a bridle, in very much the attitude of young Alexander curbing the fiery Bucephalus.[7] A superb figure, tossed up as by the horns of Taurus against the thunderous sky, cheerily hallooing to the strenuous file along the spar.

The moral nature was seldom out of keeping with the physical make. Indeed, except as toned by the former, the comeliness and power, always attractive in masculine conjunction, hardly could have drawn the sort of honest homage the Handsome Sailor in some examples received from his less gifted associates.

Such a cynosure, at least in aspect, and something such too in nature, though with important variations made apparent as the story proceeds, was welkin-eyed[8] Billy Budd—or Baby Budd, as more familiarly, under circumstances hereafter to be given, he at last came to be called—aged twenty-one, a foretopman of the British fleet toward the close of the last decade of the eighteenth century. It was not very long prior to the time of the narration that follows that he had entered the King's service, having been impressed on the Narrow Seas[9] from a homeward-bound

4

English merchantman into a seventy-four outward bound, H.M.S. *Bellipotent;*[10] which ship, as was not unusual in those hurried days, having been obliged to put to sea short of her proper complement of men. Plump upon Billy at first sight in the gangway the boarding officer, Lieutenant Ratcliffe, pounced, even before the merchantman's crew was formally mustered on the quarter-deck for his deliberate inspection. And him only he elected. For whether it was because the other men when ranged before him showed to ill advantage after Billy, or whether he had some scruples in view of the merchantman's being rather short-handed, however it might be, the officer contented himself with his first spontaneous choice. To the surprise of the ship's company, though much to the lieutenant's satisfaction, Billy made no demur. But, indeed, any demur would have been as idle as the protest of a goldfinch popped into a cage.

Noting this uncomplaining acquiescence, all but cheerful, one might say, the shipmaster[11] turned a surprised glance of silent reproach at the sailor. The shipmaster was one of those worthy mortals found in every vocation, even the humbler ones—the sort of person whom everybody agrees in calling "a respectable man." And—nor so strange to report as it may appear to be—though a ploughman of the troubled waters, lifelong contending with the intractable elements, there was nothing this honest soul at heart loved better than simple peace and quiet. For the rest, he was fifty or thereabouts, a little inclined to corpulence, a prepossessing face, unwhiskered, and of an agreeable color—a rather full face, humanely intelligent in expression. On a fair day with a fair wind and all going well, a certain musical chime in his voice seemed to be the veritable unobstructed outcome of the innermost man. He had much prudence, much conscientiousness, and there were occasions when these virtues were the cause of overmuch disquietude in him. On a passage, so long as his craft was in any proximity to land, no sleep for Captain Graveling. He took to heart those serious responsibilities not so heavily borne by some shipmasters.

Now while Billy Budd was down in the forecastle getting his kit together, the *Bellipotent*'s lieutenant, burly and bluff, nowise disconcerted by Captain Graveling's omitting to proffer the customary hospitalities on an occasion so unwelcome to him, an omission simply caused by preoccupation of thought, unceremoniously invited himself into the cabin, and also to a flask from the spirit locker, a receptacle which his experienced eye instantly discovered. In fact he was one of those sea dogs in whom all the hardship and peril of naval life in the great prolonged wars of his time never impaired the natural instinct for sensuous enjoyment. His duty he always faithfully did; but duty is sometimes a dry obligation, and he was for irrigating its aridity, whensoever possible, with a fertilizing decoction of strong waters. For the cabin's proprietor there was nothing left but to play the part of the enforced host with whatever grace and alacrity were practicable. As necessary adjuncts to the flask, he silently placed tumbler and water jug before the irrepressible guest. But excusing himself from partaking just then, he dismally watched the unembarrassed officer deliberately diluting his grog a little, then tossing it off in three swallows, pushing the empty tumbler away, yet not so far as to be beyond easy reach, at the same time settling himself in his seat and smacking his lips with high satisfaction, looking straight at the host.

These proceedings over, the master broke the silence; and there lurked a rueful reproach in the tone of his voice: "Lieutenant, you are going to take my best man from me, the jewel of 'em."

"Yes, I know," rejoined the other, immediately drawing back the tumbler preliminary to a replenishing. "Yes, I know. Sorry."

"Beg pardon, but you don't understand, Lieutenant. See here, now. Before I shipped that young fellow, my forecastle was a rat-pit of quarrels. It was black times, I tell you, aboard the *Rights* here. I was worried to that degree my pipe had no comfort for me. But Billy came; and it was like a Catholic priest striking peace in an Irish shindy.[12] Not that he preached to them or said or did anything in

6

particular; but a virtue went out of him, sugaring the sour ones. They took to him like hornets to treacle; all but the buffer of the gang, the big shaggy chap with the fire-red whiskers. He indeed, out of envy, perhaps, of the newcomer, and thinking such a "sweet and pleasant fellow," as he mockingly designated him to the others, could hardly have the spirit of a gamecock, must needs bestir himself in trying to get up an ugly row with him. Billy forebore with him and reasoned with him in a pleasant way—he is something like myself, Lieutenant, to whom aught like a quarrel is hateful—but nothing served. So, in the second dogwatch one day, the Red Whiskers in presence of the others, under pretense of showing Billy just whence a sirloin steak was cut—for the fellow had once been a butcher—insultingly gave him a dig under the ribs. Quick as lightning Billy let fly his arm. I dare say he never meant to do quite as much as he did, but anyhow he gave the burly fool a terrible drubbing. It took about half a minute, I should think. And, lord bless you, the lubber was astonished at the celerity. And will you believe it, Lieutenant, the Red Whiskers now really loves Billy—loves him, or is the biggest hypocrite that ever I heard of. But they all love him. Some of 'em do his washing, darn his old trousers for him; the carpenter is at odd times making a pretty little chest of drawers for him. Anybody will do anything for Billy Budd; and it's the happy family here. But now, Lieutenant, if that young fellow goes—I know how it will be aboard the *Rights*. Not again very soon shall I, coming up from dinner, lean over the capstan smoking a quiet pipe—no, not very soon again, I think. Ay, Lieutenant, you are going to take away the jewel of 'em; you are going to take away my peacemaker!" And with that the good soul had really some ado in checking a rising sob.

"Well," said the lieutenant, who had listened with amused interest to all this and now was waxing merry with his tipple; "well, blessed are the peacemakers, especially the fighting peacemakers. And such are the seventy-four beauties some of which you see poking their noses out of the portholes of yonder warship lying to for me," pointing through the cabin window at the *Bellipotent*. "But courage! Don't look so downhearted, man. Why, I pledge you in advance the royal approbation. Rest assured that His Majesty will be delighted to know that in a time when his hardtack is not sought for by sailors with such avidity as should be, a time also when some shipmasters privily resent the borrowing from them a tar or two for the service; His Majesty, I say, will be delighted to learn that *one* shipmaster at least cheerfully surrenders to the King the flower of his flock, a sailor who with equal loyalty makes no dissent.—But where's my beauty? Ah," looking through the cabin's open door, "here he comes; and, by Jove, lugging along his chest—Apollo with his portmanteau!—My man," stepping out to him, "you can't take that big box aboard a warship. The boxes there are mostly shot boxes. Put your duds in a bag, lad. Boot and saddle for the cavalryman, bag and hammock for the man-of-war's man."

The transfer from chest to bag was made. And, after seeing his man into the cutter and then following him down, the lieutenant pushed off from the *Rights-of-Man*.[13] That was the merchant ship's name, though by her master and crew abbreviated in sailor fashion into the *Rights*. The hard-headed Dundee owner was a staunch admirer of Thomas Paine, whose book in rejoinder to Burke's arraignment of the French Revolution had then been published for some time and had gone everywhere. In christening his vessel after the title of Paine's volume the man of Dundee was something like his contemporary shipowner, Stephen Girard of Philadelphia, whose sympathies, alike with his native land and its liberal philosophers, he evinced by naming his ships after Voltaire, Diderot, and so forth.[14]

But now, when the boat swept under the merchantman's stern, and officer and oarsmen were noting—some bitterly and others with a grin—the name emblazoned there; just then it was that the new recruit jumped up from the bow where the coxswain had directed him to sit, and waving hat to his silent shipmates sorrowfully looking over at him from the taffrail, bade the lads a genial good-bye.

Then, making a salutation as to the ship herself, "And good-bye to you too, old *Rights-of-Man*."

"Down, sir!" roared the lieutenant, instantly assuming all the rigor of his rank, though with difficulty repressing a smile.

To be sure, Billy's action was a terrible breach of naval decorum. But in that decorum he had never been instructed; in consideration of which the lieutenant would hardly have been so energetic in reproof but for the concluding farewell to the ship. This he rather took as meant to convey a covert sally on the new recruit's part, a sly slur at impressment in general, and that of himself in especial. And yet, more likely, if satire it was in effect, it was hardly so by intention, for Billy, though happily endowed with the gaiety of high health, youth, and a free heart, was yet by no means of a satirical turn. The will to it and the sinister dexterity[15] were alike wanting. To deal in double meanings and insinuations of any sort was quite foreign to his nature.

As to his enforced enlistment, that he seemed to take pretty much as he was wont to take any vicissitude of weather. Like the animals, though no philosopher, he was, without knowing it, practically a fatalist. And it may be that he rather liked this adventurous turn in his affairs, which promised an opening into novel scenes and martial excitements.

Aboard the *Bellipotent* our merchant sailor was forthwith rated as an able seaman and assigned to the starboard watch of the foretop.[16] He was soon at home in the service, not at all disliked for his unpretentious good looks and a sort of genial happy-go-lucky air. No merrier man in his mess:[17] in marked contrast to certain other individuals included like himself among the impressed portion of the ship's company; for these when not actively employed were sometimes, and more particularly in the last dogwatch[18] when the drawing near of twilight induced revery, apt to fall into a saddish mood which in some partook of sullenness. But they were not so young as our foretopman, and no few of them must have known a hearth of some sort, others may have had wives and children left, too probably, in uncertain circumstances, and hardly any but must have had acknowledged kith and kin, while for Billy, as will shortly be seen, his entire family was practically invested in himself.

2

Though our new-made foretopman was well received in the top and on the gun decks, hardly here was he that cynosure he had previously been among those minor ship's companies of the merchant marine, with which companies only had he hitherto consorted.

He was young; and despite his all but fully developed frame, in aspect looked even younger than he really was, owing to a lingering adolescent expression in the as yet smooth face all but feminine in purity of natural complexion but where, thanks to his seagoing, the lily was quite suppressed and the rose had some ado visibly to flush through the tan.

To one essentially such a novice in the complexities of factitious life, the abrupt transition from his former and simpler sphere to the ampler and more knowing world of a great warship; this might well have abashed him had there been any conceit or vanity in his composition. Among her miscellaneous multitude, the *Bellipotent* mustered several individuals who however inferior in grade were of no common natural stamp, sailors more signally susceptive of that air which continuous martial discipline and repeated presence in battle can in some degree impart even to the average man. As the Handsome Sailor, Billy Budd's position aboard the seventy-four was something analogous to that of a rustic beauty transplanted from the provinces and brought into competition with the highborn dames of the court. But this change of circumstances he scarce noted. As little did he observe that something about him provoked an ambiguous smile in one or two harder faces among the bluejackets. Nor less unaware was he of the peculiar favorable effect his person and demeanor had upon the more intelligent gentlemen of the quarter-deck. Nor could this well have been otherwise. Cast in a mold peculiar to the finest physical examples of those Englishmen in whom the Saxon strain would seem not at all to partake of any Norman or other admixture, he showed in face that humane look of reposeful good nature which the Greek sculptor in some instances gave to his heroic strong man, Hercules. But this again was subtly modified by another and pervasive quality. The ear, small and shapely, the arch of the foot, the curve in mouth and nostril, even the indurated hand dyed to the orange-tawny of the toucan's bill, a hand telling alike of the halyards and tar bucket; but, above all, something in the mobile expression, and every chance attitude and movement, something suggestive of a mother eminently favored by Love and the Graces; all this strangely indicated a lineage in direct contradiction to his lot. The mysteriousness here became less mysterious through a matter of fact elicited when Billy at the capstan was being formally mustered into the service. Asked by the officer, a small, brisk little gentleman as it chanced, among other questions, his place of birth, he replied, "Please, sir, I don't know."

"Don't know where you were born? Who was your father?"

"God knows, sir."

Struck by the straightforward simplicity of these replies, the officer next asked, "Do you know anything about your beginning?"

"No, sir. But I have heard that I was found in a pretty silk-lined basket hanging one morning from the knocker of a good man's door in Bristol."

"*Found*, say you? Well," throwing back his head and looking up and down the new recruit; "well, it turns out to have been a pretty good find. Hope they'll find some more like you, my man; the fleet sadly needs them."

Yes, Billy Budd was a foundling, a presumable by-blow,[1] and, evidently, no ignoble one. Noble descent was as evident in him as in a blood horse.

For the rest, with little or no sharpness of faculty or any trace of the wisdom of the serpent, nor yet quite a dove,[2] he possessed that kind and degree of intelligence going along with the unconventional rectitude of a sound human creature, one to whom not yet has been proffered the questionable apple of knowledge. He was illiterate; he could not read, but he could sing, and like the illiterate nightingale was sometimes the composer of his own song.

Of self-consciousness he seemed to have little or none, or about as much as we may reasonably impute to a dog of Saint Bernard's breed.

Habitually living with the elements and knowing little more of the land than as a beach, or, rather, that portion of the terraqueous globe providentially set apart for dance-houses, doxies,[3] and tapsters, in short what sailors call a "fiddler's green," his simple nature remained unsophisticated by those moral obliquities which are not in every case incompatible with that manufacturable thing known as respectability. But are sailors, frequenters of fiddlers' greens, without vices? No; but less often than with landsmen do their vices, so called, partake of crookedness of heart, seeming less to proceed from viciousness than exuberance of vitality after long constraint: frank manifestations in accordance with natural law. By his original constitution aided by the co-operating influences of his lot, Billy in many respects was little more than a sort of upright barbarian, much such perhaps as Adam presumably might have been ere the urbane Serpent wriggled himself into his company.

And here be it submitted that apparently going to corroborate the doctrine of man's Fall, a doctrine now popularly ignored, it is observable that where certain virtues pristine and unadulterate peculiarly characterize anybody in the external uniform of civilization, they will upon scrutiny seem not to be derived from custom or convention, but rather to be out of keeping with these, as if indeed exceptionally transmitted from a period prior to Cain's city and citified man.[4] The character marked by such qualities has to an unvitiated taste an untampered-with flavor like that of berries, while the man thoroughly civilized, even in a fair specimen of the breed, has to the same moral palate a questionable smack as of a compounded wine. To any stray inheritor of these primitive qualities found, like Caspar Hauser,[5] wandering dazed in any Christian capital of our time, the good-natured poet's famous invocation, near two thousand years ago, of the good rustic out of his latitude in the Rome of the Caesars, still appropriately holds:

> Honest and poor, faithful in word and thought,
> What hath thee, Fabian, to the city brought?[6]

Though our Handsome Sailor had as much of masculine beauty as one can expect anywhere to see; nevertheless, like the beautiful woman in one of Hawthorne's minor tales,[7] there was just one thing amiss in him. No visible blemish indeed, as with the lady; no, but an occasional liability to a vocal defect. Though in the hour of elemental uproar or peril he was everything that a sailor should be, yet under sudden provocation of strong heart-feeling his voice, otherwise singularly musical, as if expressive of the harmony within, was apt to develop an organic hesitancy, in fact more or less of a stutter or even worse. In this particular Billy was a striking instance that the arch interferer, the envious marplot of Eden,[8] still has more or less to do with every human consignment to this planet of Earth. In every case, one way or another he is sure to slip in his little card, as much as to remind us—I too have a hand here.

The avowal of such an imperfection in the Handsome Sailor should be evidence not alone that he is not presented as a conventional hero, but also that the story in which he is the main figure is no romance.

3

At the time of Billy Budd's arbitrary enlistment into the *Bellipotent* that ship was on her way to join the Mediterranean fleet. No long time elapsed before the junction was effected. As one of that fleet the seventy-four participated in its movements, though at times on account of her superior sailing qualities, in the absence of frigates, dispatched on separate duty as a scout and at times on less temporary service. But with all this the story has little concernment, restricted as it is to the inner life of one particular ship and the career of an individual sailor.

It was the summer of 1797. In the April of that year had occurred the commotion at Spithead followed in May by a second and yet more serious outbreak in the fleet at the Nore.[1] The latter is known, and without exaggeration in the epithet, as "the Great Mutiny." It was indeed a demonstration more menacing to England than the contemporary manifestoes and conquering and proselyting armies of the French Directory.[2] To the British Empire the Nore Mutiny was what a strike in the fire brigade would be to London threatened by general arson. In a crisis when the kingdom might well have anticipated the famous signal[3] that some years later published along the naval line of battle what it was that upon occasion England expected of Englishmen; *that* was the time when at the mastheads of the three-deckers and seventy-fours moored in her own roadstead[4]—a fleet the right arm of a Power then all but the sole free conservative one of the Old World—the bluejackets, to be numbered by thousands, ran up with huzzas the British colors with the union and cross wiped out; by that cancellation transmuting the flag of founded law and freedom defined, into the enemy's red meteor of unbridled and unbounded revolt. Reasonable discontent growing out of practical grievances in the fleet had been ignited into irrational combusion as by live cinders blown across the Channel from France in flames.[5]

The event converted into irony for a time those spirited strains of Dibdin[6]—as a song-writer no mean auxiliary to the English government at that European conjuncture—strains celebrating, among other things, the patriotic devotion of the British tar: "And as for my life, 'tis the King's!"

Such an episode in the Island's grand naval story her naval historians naturally abridge, one of them (William James)[7] candidly acknowledging that fain would he pass it over did not "impartiality forbid fastidiousness." And yet

14

his mention is less a narration than a reference, having to do hardly at all with details. Nor are these readily to be found in the libraries. Like some other events in every age befalling states everywhere, including America, the Great Mutiny was of such character that national pride along with views of policy would fain shade it off into the historical background. Such events cannot be ignored, but there is a considerate way of historically treating them. If a well-constituted individual refrains from blazoning aught amiss or calamitous in his family, a nation in the like circumstance may without reproach be equally discreet.

Though after parleyings between government and the ringleaders, and concessions by the former as to some glaring abuses, the first uprising—that at Spithead—with difficulty was put down, or matters for the time pacified; yet at the Nore the unforeseen renewal of insurrection on a yet larger scale, and emphasized in the conferences that ensued by demands deemed by the authorities not only inadmissible but aggressively insolent, indicated—if the Red Flag[8] did not sufficiently do so—what was the spirit animating the men. Final suppression, however, there was; but only made possible perhaps by the unswerving loyalty of the marine corps and a voluntary resumption of loyalty among influential sections of the crews.

To some extent the Nore Mutiny may be regarded as analogous to the distempering irruption of contagious fever in a frame constitutionally sound, and which anon throws it off.

At all events, of these thousands of mutineers were some of the tars who not so very long afterwards—whether wholly prompted thereto by patriotism, or pugnacious instinct, or by both—helped to win a coronet for Nelson at the Nile, and the naval crown of crowns for him at Trafalgar.[9] To the mutineers, those battles and especially Trafalgar were a plenary absolution and a grand one. For all that goes to make up scenic naval display and heroic magnificence in arms, those battles, especially Trafalgar, stand unmatched in human annals.

4

In this matter of writing, resolve as one may to keep to the main road, some bypaths have an enticement not readily to be withstood. I am going to err into such a bypath. If the reader will keep me company I shall be glad. At the least, we can promise ourselves that pleasure which is wickedly said to be in sinning, for a literary sin the divergence will be.

Very likely it is no new remark that the inventions of our time have at last brought about a change in sea warfare in degree corresponding to the revolution in all warfare effected by the original introduction from China into Europe of gunpowder. The first European firearm, a clumsy contrivance, was, as is well known, scouted by no few of the knights as a base implement, good enough peradventure for weavers too craven to stand up crossing steel with steel in frank fight. But as ashore knightly valor, though shorn of its blazonry, did not cease with the knights, neither on the seas—though nowadays in encounters there a certain kind of displayed gallantry be fallen out of date as hardly applicable under changed circumstances—did the nobler qualities of such naval magnates as Don John of Austria, Doria, Van Tromp, Jean Bart, the long line of British admirals, and the American Decaturs of 1812[1] become obsolete with their wooden walls.

Nevertheless, to anybody who can hold the Present at its worth without being inappreciative of the Past, it may be forgiven, if to such an one the solitary old hulk at Portsmouth, Nelson's *Victory,* seems to float there, not alone as the decaying monument of a fame incorruptible, but also as a poetic reproach, softened by its picturesqueness, to the *Monitors*[2] and yet mightier hulls of the European ironclads. And this not altogether because such craft are unsightly, unavoidably lacking the symmetry and grand lines of the old battleships, but equally for other reasons.

There are some, perhaps, who while not altogether

inaccessible to that poetic reproach just alluded to, may yet on behalf of the new order be disposed to parry it; and this to the extent of iconoclasm, if need be. For example, prompted by the sight of the star inserted in the *Victory's* quarter-deck designating the spot where the Great Sailor fell, these martial utilitarians may suggest considerations implying that Nelson's ornate publication of his person in battle was not only unnecessary, but not military, nay, savored of foolhardiness and vanity. They may add, too, that at Trafalgar it was in effect nothing less than a challenge to death; and death came; and that but for his bravado the victorious admiral might possibly have survived the battle, and so, instead of having his sagacious dying injunctions overruled by his immediate successor in command, he himself when the contest was decided might have brought his shattered fleet to anchor, a proceeding which might have averted the deplorable loss of life by shipwreck in the elemental tempest that followed the martial one.

Well, should we set aside the more than disputable point whether for various reasons it was possible to anchor the fleet, then plausibly enough the Benthamites of war[3] may urge the above. But the *might-have-been* is but boggy ground to build on. And, certainly, in foresight as to the larger issue of an encounter, and anxious preparations for it—buoying the deadly way and mapping it out, as at Copenhagen[4]—few commanders have been so painstakingly circumspect as this same reckless declarer of his person in fight.

Personal prudence, even when dictated by quite other than selfish considerations, surely is no special virtue in a military man; while an excessive love of glory, impassioning a less burning impulse, the honest sense of duty, is the first. If the name *Wellington*[5] is not so much of a trumpet to the blood as the simpler name *Nelson,* the reason for this may perhaps be inferred from the above. Alfred in his funeral ode[6] on the victor of Waterloo ventures not to call him the greatest soldier of all time, though in the same ode he invokes Nelson as "the greatest sailor since our world began."

At Trafalgar Nelson on the brink of opening the fight sat down and wrote his last brief will and testament. If under the presentiment of the most magnificent of all victories to be crowned by his own glorious death, a sort of priestly motive led him to dress his person in the jewelled vouchers of his own shining deeds; if thus to have adorned himself for the altar and the sacrifice were indeed vainglory, then affectation and fustian is each more heroic line in the great epics and dramas, since in such lines the poet but embodies in verse those exaltations of sentiment that a nature like Nelson, the opportunity being given, vitalizes into acts.

5

Yes, the outbreak at the Nore was put down. But not every grievance was redressed. If the contractors, for example, were no longer permitted to ply some practices peculiar to their tribe everywhere, such as providing shoddy cloth, rations not sound, or false in the measure; not the less impressment, for one thing, went on. By custom sanctioned for centuries, and judicially maintained by a Lord Chancellor as late as Mansfield,[1] that mode of manning the fleet, a mode now fallen into a sort of abeyance but never formally renounced, it was not practicable to give up in those years. Its abrogation would have crippled the indispensable fleet, one wholly under canvas, no steam power, its innumerable sails and thousands of cannon, everything in short, worked by muscle alone; a fleet the more insatiate in demand for men, because then multiplying its ships of all grades against contingencies present and to come of the convulsed Continent.

Discontent foreran the Two Mutinies,[2] and more or less it lurkingly survived them. Hence it was not unreasonable to apprehend some return of trouble sporadic or general. One instance of such apprehensions: In the same year with this story, Nelson, then Rear Admiral Sir Horatio, being with the fleet off the Spanish coast, was directed by the admiral in command to shift his pennant[3] from the *Captain* to the *Theseus*; and for this reason: that the latter ship having newly arrived on the station from home, where it had taken part in the Great Mutiny, danger was apprehended from the temper of the men; and it was thought that an officer like Nelson was the one, not indeed to terrorize the crew into base subjection, but to win them, by force of his mere presence and heroic personality, back to an allegiance if not as enthusiastic as his own yet as true.

So it was that for a time, on more than one quarter-deck, anxiety did exist. At sea, precautionary vigilance was strained against relapse. At short notice an engagement might come on. When it did, the lieutenants assigned to batteries felt it incumbent on them, in some instances, to stand with drawn swords behind the men working the guns.

6

But on board the seventy-four in which Billy now swung his hammock, very little in the manner of the men and nothing obvious in the demeanor of the officers would have suggested to an ordinary observer that the Great Mutiny was a recent event. In their general bearing and conduct the commissioned officers of a warship naturally take their tone from the commander, that is if he have that ascendancy of character that ought to be his.

Captain the Honorable Edward Fairfax Vere,[1] to give his full title, was a bachelor of forty or thereabouts, a sailor of distinction even in a time prolific of renowned seamen. Though allied to the higher nobility, his advancement had not been altogether owing to influences connected with that circumstance. He had seen much service, been in various engagements, always acquitting himself as an officer mindful of the welfare of his men, but never tolerating an infraction of discipline; thoroughly versed in the science of his profession, and intrepid to the verge of temerity, though never injudiciously so. For his gallantry in the West Indian waters as flag lieutenant under Rodney in that admiral's crowning victory over De Grasse,[2] he was made a post captain.

Ashore, in the garb of a civilian, scarce anyone would have taken him for a sailor, more especially that he never garnished unprofessional talk with nautical terms, and grave in his bearing, evinced little appreciation of mere humor. It was not out of keeping with these traits that on a passage when nothing demanded his paramount action, he was the most undemonstrative of men. Any landsman observing this gentleman not conspicuous by his stature and wearing no pronounced insignia, emerging from his cabin to the open deck, and noting the silent deference of the officers retiring to leeward, might have taken him for the King's guest, a civilian aboard the King's ship, some highly honorable discreet envoy on his way to an important post. But in fact this unobtrusiveness of demeanor may have proceeded from a certain unaffected modesty of manhood sometimes accompanying a resolute nature, a modesty evinced at all times not calling for pronounced action, which shown in any rank of life suggests a virtue aristocratic in kind. As with some others engaged in various departments of the world's more heroic activities, Captain Vere though practical enough upon occasion would at times betray a certain dreaminess of mood. Standing alone on the weather side of the quarter-deck, one hand holding by the rigging, he would absently gaze off at the blank sea.[3] At the presentation to him then of some minor matter interrupting the current of his thoughts, he would show more or less irascibility; but instantly he would control it.

In the navy he was popularly known by the appellation "Starry Vere." How such a designation happened to fall upon one who whatever his sterling qualities was without any brilliant ones, was in this wise: A favorite kinsman, Lord Denton, a freehearted fellow, had been the first to meet and congratulate him upon his return to England from his West Indian cruise; and but the day previous turning over a copy of Andrew Marvell's[4] poems had lighted, not for the first time, however, upon the lines entitled "Appleton House," the name of one of the seats of their common ancestor, a hero in the German wars of the seventeenth century, in which poem occur the lines:

> This 'tis to have been from the first
> In a domestic heaven nursed,
> Under the discipline severe
> Of Fairfax and the starry Vere.[5]

And so, upon embracing his cousin fresh from Rodney's great victory wherein he had played so gallant a part, brimming over with just family pride in the sailor of their house, he exuberantly exclaimed, "Give ye joy, Ed; give ye joy, my starry Vere!" This got currency, and the novel prefix serving in familiar parlance readily to distinguish the *Bellipotent*'s captain from another Vere his senior, a distant relative, an officer of like rank in the navy, it remained permanently attached to the surname.

7

In view of the part that the commander of the *Bellipotent* plays in scenes shortly to follow, it may be well to fill out that sketch of him outlined in the previous chapter.

Aside from his qualities as a sea officer Captain Vere was an exceptional character. Unlike no few of England's renowned sailors, long and arduous service with signal devotion to it had not resulted in absorbing and *salting* the entire man. He had a marked leaning toward everything intellectual. He loved books, never going to sea without a newly replenished library, compact but of the best. The isolated leisure, in some cases so wearisome, falling at intervals to commanders even during a war cruise, never was tedious to Captain Vere. With nothing of that literary taste which less heeds the thing conveyed than the vehicle, his bias was toward those books to which every serious mind of superior order occupying any active post of authority in the world naturally inclines: books treating of actual men and events no matter of what era—history, biography, and unconventional writers like Montaigne,[1] who, free from cant and convention, honestly and in the spirit of common sense philosophize upon realities. In this line of reading he found confirmation of his own more reserved thoughts—confirmation which he had vainly sought in social converse, so that as touching most fundamental topics, there had got to be established in him some positive convictions which he forefelt would abide in him essentially unmodified so long as his intelligent part remained unimpaired. In view of the troubled period in which his lot was cast, this was well for him. His settled convictions were as a dike against those invading waters of novel opinion social, political, and otherwise, which carried away as in a torrent no few minds in those days, minds by nature not inferior to his own. While other members of that aristocracy to which by birth he belonged were incensed at the innovators mainly because their theories were inimical to the privileged classes, Captain Vere disinterestedly opposed them not alone because they seemed to him insusceptible of embodiment in lasting institutions, but at war with the peace of the world and the true welfare of mankind.

With minds less stored than his and less earnest, some officers of his rank, with whom at times he would necessarily consort, found him lacking in the companionable quality, a dry and bookish gentleman, as they deemed. Upon any chance withdrawal from their company one would be apt to say to another something like this: "Vere is a noble fellow, Starry Vere. 'Spite the gazettes, Sir Horatio" (meaning him who became Lord Nelson) "is at bottom scarce a better seaman or fighter. But between you and me now, don't you think there is a queer streak of the pedantic running through him? Yes, like the King's yarn in a coil of navy rope?"

Some apparent ground there was for this sort of confidential criticism; since not only did the captain's discourse never fall into the jocosely familiar, but in illustrating of any point touching the stirring personages and events of the time he would be as apt to cite some historic character or incident of antiquity as he would be to cite from the moderns. He seemed unmindful of the circumstance that to his bluff company such remote allusions, however pertinent they might really be, were altogether alien to men whose reading was mainly confined to the journals.[2] But considerateness in such matters is not easy to natures constituted like Captain Vere's. Their honesty prescribes to them directness, sometimes far-reaching like that of a migratory fowl that in its flight never heeds when it crosses a frontier.

8

The lieutenants and other commissioned gentlemen forming Captain Vere's staff it is not necessary here to particularize, nor needs it to make any mention of any of the warrant officers. But among the petty officers[1] was one who, having much to do with the story, may as well be forthwith introduced. His portrait I essay, but shall never hit it. This was John Claggart, the master-at-arms. But that sea title may to landsmen seem somewhat equivocal. Originally, doubtless, that petty officer's function was the instruction of the men in the use of arms, sword or cutlass. But very long ago, owing to the advance in gunnery making hand-to-hand encounters less frequent and giving to niter and sulphur the pre-eminence over steel, that function ceased; the master-at-arms of a great warship becoming a sort of chief of police charged among other matters with the duty of preserving order on the populous lower gun decks.

Claggart was a man about five-and-thirty, somewhat spare and tall, yet of no ill figure upon the whole. His hand was too small and shapely to have been accustomed to hard toil. The face was a notable one, the features all except the chin cleanly cut as those on a Greek medallion; yet the chin, beardless as Tecumseh's,[2] had something of strange protuberant broadness in its make that recalled the prints of the Reverend Dr. Titus Oates,[3] the historic deponent with the clerical drawl in the time of Charles II and the fraud of the alleged Popish Plot. It served Claggart in his office that his eye could cast a tutoring glance. His brow was of the sort phrenologically associated[4] with more than average intellect; silken jet curls partly clustering over it, making a foil to the pallor below, a pallor tinged with a faint shade of amber akin to the hue of time-tinted marbles of old. This complexion, singularly contrasting with the red or deeply bronzed visages of the sailors, and in part the result of his official seclusion from the sunlight, though it was not exactly displeasing, nevertheless seemed to hint of something defective or abnormal in the constitution and blood. But his general aspect and manner were so suggestive of an education and career incongruous with his naval function that when not actively engaged in it he looked like a man of high quality, social and moral, who for reasons of his own was keeping incog.[5] Nothing was known of his former life. It might be that he was an Englishman; and yet there lurked a bit of accent in his speech suggesting that possibly he was not such by birth, but through naturalization in early childhood. Among certain grizzled sea gossips of the gun decks and forecastle went a rumor perdue that the master-at-arms was a *chevalier*[6] who had volunteered into the King's navy by way of compounding for some mysterious swindle whereof he had been arraigned at the King's Bench.[7] The fact that nobody could substantiate this report was, of course, nothing against its secret currency. Such a rumor once started on the gun decks in reference to almost anyone below the rank of a commissioned officer would, during the period assigned to this narrative, have seemed not altogether wanting in credibility to the tarry old wiseacres of a man-of-war crew. And indeed a man of Claggart's accomplishments, without prior nautical experience entering the navy at mature life, as he did, and necessarily allotted at the start to the lowest grade in it; a man too who never made allusion to his previous life ashore; these were circumstances which in the dearth of exact knowledge as to his true antecedents opened to the invidious a vague field for unfavorable surmise.

But the sailors' dogwatch gossip concerning him derived a vague plausibility from the fact that now for some period the British navy could so little afford to be squeamish in the matter of keeping up the muster rolls, that not only were press gangs[8] notoriously abroad both afloat and ashore, but there was little or no secret about another matter, namely, that the London police were at liberty to capture any able-bodied suspect, any questionable fellow at large, and summarily ship him to the dockyard or fleet. Furthermore, even among voluntary enlistments there were instances where the motive thereto partook neither of patriotic impulse nor yet of a random desire to experience a bit of sea life and martial adventure. Insolvent debtors of minor grade, together with the promiscuous lame ducks of morality, found in the navy a convenient and secure refuge, secure because, once enlisted aboard a King's ship, they were as much in sanctuary as the transgressor of the Middle Ages harboring himself under the shadow of the altar. Such sanctioned irregularities, which for obvious reasons the government would hardly think to parade at the time and which consequently, and as affecting the least influential class of mankind, have all but dropped into oblivion, lend color to something for the truth whereof I do not vouch, and hence have some scruple in stating; something I remember having seen in print though the book I cannot recall; but the same thing was personally communicated to me now more than forty years ago by an old pensioner in a cocked hat with whom I had a most interesting talk on the terrace at Greenwich, a Baltimore Negro, a Trafalgar man.[9] It was to this effect: In the case of a warship short of hands whose speedy sailing was imperative, the deficient quota, in lack of any other way of making it good, would be eked out by drafts culled direct from the jails. For reasons previously suggested it would not perhaps be easy at the present day directly to prove or disprove the allegation. But allowed as a verity, how significant would it be of England's straits at the time confronted by those wars which like a flight of harpies[10] rose shrieking from the din and dust of the fallen Bastille.[11] That era appears measurably clear to us who look back at it, and but read of it. But to the grandfathers of us graybeards, the more thoughtful of them, the genius of it presented an aspect like that of Camoëns' Spirit of the Cape,[12] an eclipsing menace mysterious and prodigious. Not America was exempt from apprehension. At the height of Napoleon's unexampled conquests, there were Americans who had fought at Bunker Hill[13] who looked forward to the possibility that the Atlantic might prove no barrier against the ultimate schemes of this French portentous upstart from the revolutionary chaos who seemed in act of fulfilling judgment prefigured in the Apocalypse.[14]

But the less credence was to be given to the gun-deck talk touching Claggart, seeing that no man holding his office in a man-of-war can ever hope to be popular with the crew. Besides, in derogatory comments upon anyone against whom they have a grudge, or for any reason or no reason mislike, sailors are much like landsmen: they are apt to exaggerate or romance it.

About as much was really known to the *Bellipotent*'s tars of the master-at-arms' career before entering the service as an astronomer knows about a comet's travels prior to its first observable appearance in the sky. The verdict of the sea quidnuncs[15] has been cited only by way of showing what sort of moral impression the man made upon rude uncultivated natures whose conceptions of human wickedness were necessarily of the narrowest, limited to ideas of vulgar rascality—a thief among the swinging hammocks during a night watch, or the man-brokers and land-sharks of the seaports.

It was no gossip, however, but fact that though, as before hinted, Claggart upon his entrance into the navy was, as a novice, assigned to the least honorable section[16] of a man-of-war's crew, embracing the drudgery, he did not long remain there. The superior capacity he immediately evinced, his constitutional sobriety, an ingratiating deference to superiors, together with a peculiar ferreting genius manifested on a singular occasion; all this, capped by a certain austere patriotism, abruptly advanced him to the position of master-at-arms.

Of this maritime chief of police the ship's corporals, so called, were the immediate subordinates, and compliant ones; and this, as is to be noted in some business departments ashore, almost to a degree inconsistent with entire moral volition. His place put various converging wires of underground influence under the chief's control, capable when astutely worked through his understrappers of operating to the mysterious discomfort, if nothing worse, of any of the sea commonalty.

9

Life in the foretop well agreed with Billy Budd. There, when not actually engaged on the yards yet higher aloft, the topmen, who as such had been picked out for youth and activity, constituted an aerial club lounging at ease against the smaller stun'sails rolled up into cushions, spinning yarns like the lazy gods, and frequently amused with what was going on in the busy world of the decks below. No wonder then that a young fellow of Billy's disposition was well content in such society. Giving no cause of offense to anybody, he was always alert at a call. So in the merchant service it had been with him. But now such a punctiliousness in duty was shown that his topmates would sometimes good-naturedly laugh at him for it. This heightened alacrity had its cause, namely, the impression made upon him by the first formal gangway-punishment he had ever witnessed, which befell the day following his impressment. It had been incurred by a little fellow, young, a novice afterguardsman[1] absent from his assigned post when the ship was being put about; a dereliction resulting in a rather serious hitch to that maneuver, one demanding instantaneous promptitude in letting go and making fast. When Billy saw the culprit's naked back under the scourge, gridironed with red welts and worse, when he marked the dire expression in the liberated man's face as with his woolen shirt flung over him by the executioner he rushed forward from the spot to bury himself in the crowd, Billy was horrified. He resolved that never through remissness would he make himself liable to such a visitation or do or omit aught that might

27

merit even verbal reproof. What then was his surprise and concern when ultimately he found himself getting into petty trouble occasionally about such matters as the stowage of his bag or something amiss in his hammock, matters under the police oversight of the ship's corporals of the lower decks, and which brought down on him a vague threat from one of them.

So heedful in all things as he was, how could this be? He could not understand it, and it more than vexed him. When he spoke to his young topmates about it they were either lightly incredulous or found something comical in his unconcealed anxiety. "Is it your bag, Billy?" said one. "Well, sew yourself up in it, bully boy, and then you'll be sure to know if anybody meddles with it."

Now there was a veteran aboard who because his years began to disqualify him for more active work had been recently assigned duty as mainmastman in his watch, looking to the gear belayed at the rail roundabout that great spar near the deck. At off-times the foretopman had picked up some acquaintance with him, and now in his trouble it occurred to him that he might be the sort of person to go to for wise counsel. He was an old Dansker[2] long anglicized in the service, of few words, many wrinkles, and some honorable scars. His wizened face, time-tinted and weather-stained to the complexion of an antique parchment, was here and there peppered blue by the chance explosion of a gun cartridge in action.

He was an *Agamemnon* man, some two years prior to the time of this story having served under Nelson when still captain in that ship immortal in naval memory, which dismantled and in part broken up to her bare ribs is seen a grand skeleton in Haden's etching.[3] As one of a boarding party from the *Agamemnon* he had received a cut slantwise along one temple and cheek leaving a long pale scar like a streak of dawn's light falling athwart the dark visage. It was on account of that scar and the affair in which it was known that he had received it, as well as from his blue-peppered complexion, that the Dansker went among the *Bellipotent*'s crew by the name of "Board-Her-in-the-Smoke."

28

Now the first time that his small weasel eyes happened to light on Billy Budd, a certain grim internal merriment set all his ancient wrinkles into antic play. Was it that his eccentric unsentimental old sapience, primitive in its kind, saw or thought it saw something which in contrast with the warship's environment looked oddly incongruous in the Handsome Sailor? But after slyly studying him at intervals, the old Merlin's[4] equivocal merriment was modified; for now when the twain would meet, it would start in his face a quizzing sort of look, but it would be but momentary and sometimes replaced by an expression of speculative query as to what might eventually befall a nature like that, dropped into a world not without some mantraps and against whose subtleties simple courage lacking experience and address, and without any touch of defensive ugliness, is of little avail; and where such innocence as man is capable of does yet in a moral emergency not always sharpen the faculties or enlighten the will.

However it was, the Dansker in his ascetic way rather took to Billy. Nor was this only because of a certain philosophic interest in such a character. There was another cause. While the old man's eccentricities, sometimes bordering on the ursine, repelled the juniors, Billy, undeterred thereby, revering him as a salt hero, would make advances, never passing the old *Agamemnon* man without a salutation marked by that respect which is seldom lost on the aged, however crabbed at times or whatever their station in life.

There was a vein of dry humor, or what not, in the mastman; and, whether in freak of patriarchal irony touching Billy's youth and athletic frame, or for some other and more recondite reason, from the first in addressing him he always substituted *Baby* for Billy, the Dansker in fact being the originator of the name by which the foretopman eventually became known aboard ship.

Well then, in his mysterious little difficulty going in quest of the wrinkled one, Billy found him off duty in a dogwatch ruminating by himself, seated on a shot box of the upper gun deck, now and then surveying with a somewhat cynical regard certain of the more swaggering promenaders there. Billy recounted his trouble, again wondering how it all happened. The salt seer attentively listened, accompanying the foretopman's recital with queer twitchings of his wrinkles and problematical little sparkles of his small ferret eyes. Making an end of his story, the foretopman asked, "And now, Dansker, do tell me what you think of it."

The old man, shoving up the front of his tarpaulin and deliberately rubbing the long slant scar at the point where it entered the thin hair, laconically said, "Baby Budd, *Jemmy Legs"* (meaning the master-at-arms) "is down on you."

"Jemmy Legs!" ejaculated Billy, his welkin eyes expanding. "What for? Why, he calls me 'the sweet and pleasant young fellow,' they tell me."

"Does he so?" grinned the grizzled one; then said, "Ay, Baby lad, a sweet voice has Jemmy Legs."

"No, not always. But to me he has. I seldom pass him but there comes a pleasant word."

"And that's because he's down upon you, Baby Budd."

Such reiteration, along with the manner of it, incomprehensible to a novice, disturbed Billy almost as much as the mystery for which he had sought explanation. Something less unpleasingly oracular he tried to extract; but the old sea Chiron,[5] thinking perhaps that for the nonce he had sufficiently instructed his young Achilles, pursed his lips, gathered all his wrinkles together, and would commit himself to nothing further.

Years, and those experiences which befall certain shrewder men subordinated lifelong to the will of superiors, all this had developed in the Dansker the pithy guarded cynicism that was his leading characteristic.

10

The next day an incident served to confirm Billy Budd in his incredulity as to the Dansker's strange summing up of the case submitted. The ship at noon, going large before the wind, was rolling on her course, and he below at dinner and engaged in some sportful talk with the members of his mess, chanced in a sudden lurch to spill the entire contents of his soup pan upon the new-scrubbed deck. Claggart, the master-at-arms, official rattan[1] in hand, happened to be passing along the battery in a bay of which the mess was lodged, and the greasy liquid streamed just across his path. Stepping over it, he was proceeding on his way without comment, since the matter was nothing to take notice of under the circumstances, when he happened to observe who it was that had done the spilling. His countenance changed. Pausing, he was about to ejaculate something hasty at the sailor, but checked himself, and pointing down to the streaming soup, playfully tapped him from behind with his rattan, saying in a low musical voice peculiar to him at times, "Handsomely done, my lad! And handsome is as handsome did it, too!" And with that passed on. Not noted by Billy as not coming within his view was the involuntary smile, or rather grimace, that accompanied Claggart's equivocal words. Aridly it drew down the thin corners of his shapely mouth. But everybody taking his remark as meant for humorous, and at which therefore as coming from a superior they were bound to laugh "with counterfeited glee,"[2] acted accordingly; and Billy, tickled, it may be, by the allusion to his being the Handsome Sailor, merrily joined in; then addressing his messmates exclaimed, "There now, who says that Jemmy Legs is down on me!"

"And who said he was, Beauty?" demanded one Donald with some surprise. Whereat the foretopman looked a little foolish, recalling that it was only one person, Board-Her-in-the-Smoke, who had suggested what to him was the smoky idea that this master-at-arms was in any peculiar way hostile to him. Meantime that functionary, resuming his path, must have momentarily worn some expression less guarded than that of the bitter smile, usurping the face from the heart—some distorting expression perhaps, for a drummer-boy heedlessly frolicking along from the opposite direction and chancing to come into light collision with his person was strangely disconcerted by his aspect. Nor was the impression lessened when the official, impetuously giving him a sharp cut with the rattan, vehemently exclaimed, "Look where you go!"

II

What was the matter with the master-at-arms? And, be the matter what it might, how could it have direct relation to Billy Budd, with whom prior to the affair of the spilled soup he had never come into any special contact official or otherwise? What indeed could the trouble have to do with one so little inclined to give offense as the merchant-ship's "peacemaker," even him who in Claggart's own phrase was "the sweet and pleasant young fellow"? Yes, why should Jemmy Legs, to borrow the Dansker's expression, be "down" on the Handsome Sailor? But, at heart and not for nothing, as the late chance encounter may indicate to the discerning, down on him, secretly down on him, he assuredly was.

Now to invent something touching the more private career of Claggart, something involving Billy Budd, of which something the latter should be wholly ignorant, some romantic incident implying that Claggart's knowledge of the young bluejacket began at some period anterior to catching sight of him on board the seventy-four— all this, not so difficult to do, might avail in a way more or less interesting to account for whatever of enigma may appear to lurk in the case. But in fact there was nothing of the sort. And yet the cause necessarily to be assumed as the sole one assignable is in its very realism as much charged with that prime element of Radcliffian romance,[1] the mysterious, as any that the ingenuity of the author of *The Mysteries of Udolpho* could devise. For what can more partake of the mysterious than an antipathy spontaneous and profound such as is evoked in certain exceptional mortals by the mere aspect of some other mortal, however harmless he may be, if not called forth by this very harmlessness itself?

Now there can exist no irritating juxtaposition of dissimilar personalities comparable to that which is possible aboard a great warship fully manned and at sea. There, every day among all ranks, almost every man comes into more or less of contact with almost every other man. Wholly there to avoid even the sight of an aggravating object one must needs give it Jonah's toss[2] or jump overboard himself. Imagine how all this might eventually operate on some peculiar human creature the direct reverse of a saint!

But for the adequate comprehending of Claggart by a normal nature these hints are insufficient. To pass from a normal nature to him one must cross "the deadly space between." And this is best done by indirection.

Long ago an honest scholar,[3] my senior, said to me in reference to one who like himself is now no more, a man so unimpeachably respectable that against him nothing was ever openly said though among the few something was whispered, "Yes, X—— is a nut not to be cracked by the tap of a lady's fan. You are aware that I am the adherent of no organized religion, much less of any philosophy built into a system. Well, for all that, I think that to try and get into X——, enter his labyrinth and get out again, without a clue derived from some source other than what is known as 'knowledge of the world'—that were hardly possible, at least for me."

"Why," said I, "X——, however singular a study to some, is yet human, and knowledge of the world assuredly implies the knowledge of human nature, and in most of its varieties."

"Yes, but a superficial knowledge of it, serving ordinary purposes. But for anything deeper, I am not certain whether to know the world and to know human nature be not two distinct branches of knowledge, which while they may coexist in the same heart, yet either may exist with little or nothing of the other. Nay, in an average man of the world, his constant rubbing with it blunts that finer spiritual insight indispensable to the understanding of the essential in certain exceptional characters, whether evil ones or good. In a matter of some importance I have seen a girl wind an old lawyer about her little finger. Nor was it the dotage of senile love. Nothing of the sort. But he knew law better than he knew the girl's heart. Coke and Blackstone[4] hardly shed so much light into obscure spiritual places as the Hebrew prophets. And who were they? Mostly recluses."

At the time, my inexperience was such that I did not quite see the drift of all this. It may be that I see it now. And, indeed, if that lexicon which is based on Holy Writ were any longer popular, one might with less difficulty define and denominate certain phenomenal men. As it is, one must turn to some authority not liable to the charge of being tinctured with the biblical element.

In a list of definitions included in the authentic translation of Plato, a list attributed to him, occurs this: "Natural Depravity:[5] a depravity according to nature," a definition which, though savoring of Calvinism,[6] by no means involves Calvin's dogma as to total mankind. Evidently its intent makes it applicable but to individuals. Not many are the examples of this depravity which the gallows and jail supply. At any rate, for notable instances, since these have no vulgar alloy of the brute in them, but invariably are dominated by intellectuality, one must go elsewhere. Civilization, especially if of the austerer sort, is auspicious to it. It folds itself in the mantle of respectability. It has its certain negative virtues serving as silent auxiliaries. It never allows wine to get within its guard. It is not going too far to say that it is without vices or small sins. There is a phenomenal pride in it that excludes them. It is never mercenary or avaricious. In short, the depravity here meant partakes nothing of the sordid or sensual. It is serious, but free from acerbity. Though no flatterer of mankind it never speaks ill of it.

But the thing which in eminent instances signalizes so exceptional a nature is this: Though the man's even temper and discreet bearing would seem to intimate a mind peculiarly subject to the law of reason, not the less in heart he would seem to riot in complete exemption from that law, having apparently little to do with reason further than to employ it as an ambidexter implement for effecting the irrational. That is to say: Toward the accomplishment of an aim which in wantonness of atrocity would seem to partake of the insane, he will direct a cool judgment sagacious and sound. These men are madmen, and of the most dangerous sort, for their lunacy is not continuous, but occasional, evoked by some special object; it is protectively secretive, which is as much as to say it is self-contained, so that when, moreover, most active it is to the average mind not distinguishable from sanity, and for the reason above suggested: that whatever its aims may be—and the aim is never declared—the method and the outward proceeding are always perfectly rational.

Now something such an one was Claggart, in whom was the mania of an evil nature, not engendered by vicious training or corrupting books or licentious living, but born with him and innate, in short "a depravity according to nature."

Dark sayings are these, some will say. But why? Is it because they somewhat savor of Holy Writ in its phrase "mystery of iniquity"?[7] If they do, such savor was far enough from being intended, for little will it commend these pages to many a reader of today.

The point of the present story turning on the hidden nature of the master-at-arms has necessitated this chapter. With an added hint or two in connection with the incident at the mess, the resumed narrative must be left to vindicate, as it may, its own credibility.

12

That Claggart's figure was not amiss, and his face, save the chin, well molded, has already been said. Of these favorable points he seemed not insensible, for he was not only neat but careful in his dress. But the form of Billy Budd was heroic; and if his face was without the intellectual look of the pallid Claggart's, not the less was it lit, like his, from within, though from a different source. The bonfire in his heart made luminous the rose-tan in his cheek.

In view of the marked contrast between the persons of the twain, it is more than probable that when the master-at-arms in the scene last given applied to the sailor the proverb "Handsome is as handsome does," he there let escape an ironic inkling, not caught by the young sailors who heard it, as to what it was that had first moved him against Billy, namely, his significant personal beauty.

Now envy and antipathy, passions irreconcilable in reason, nevertheless in fact may spring conjoined like Chang and Eng[1] in one birth. Is Envy then such a monster? Well, though many an arraigned mortal has in hopes of mitigated penalty pleaded guilty to horrible actions, did ever anybody seriously confess to envy? Something there is in it universally felt to be more shameful than even felonious crime. And not only does everybody disown it, but the better sort are inclined to incredulity when it is in earnest imputed to an intelligent man. But since its lodgment is in the heart not the brain, no degree of intellect supplies a guarantee against it. But Claggart's was no vulgar form of the passion. Nor, as directed toward Billy Budd, did it partake of that streak of apprehensive jealousy that marred Saul's visage perturbedly brooding on the comely young David.[2] Claggart's envy struck deeper. If askance he eyed the good looks, cheery health, and frank enjoyment of young life in Billy Budd, it was because these went along with a nature that, as Claggart magnetically felt, had in its simplicity never willed malice or experienced the reactionary bite of that serpent. To him, the spirit lodged within Billy, and looking out from his welkin eyes as from windows, that ineffability it was which made the dimple in his dyed cheek, suppled his joints, and dancing in his yellow curls made him preeminently the Handsome Sailor. One person excepted, the master-at-arms was perhaps the only man in the ship intellectually capable of adequately appreciating the moral phenomenon presented in Billy Budd. And the insight but intensified his passion, which assuming various secret forms within him, at times assumed that of cynic disdain, disdain of innocence—to be nothing more than innocent! Yet in an aesthetic way he saw the charm of it, the courageous free-and-easy temper of it, and fain would have shared it, but he despaired of it.

With no power to annul the elemental evil in him,

though readily enough he could hide it; apprehending the good, but powerless to be it; a nature like Claggart's, surcharged with energy as such natures almost invariably are, what recourse is left to it but to recoil upon itself and, like the scorpion for which the Creator alone is responsible, act out to the end the part allotted it.

13

Passion, and passion in its profoundest, is not a thing demanding a palatial stage whereon to play its part. Down among the groundlings,[1] among the beggars and rakers of the garbage, profound passion is enacted. And the circumstances that provoke it, however trivial or mean, are no measure of its power. In the present instance the stage is a scrubbed gun deck, and one of the external provocations a man-of-war's man's spilled soup.

Now when the master-at-arms noticed whence came that greasy fluid streaming before his feet, he must have taken it—to some extent wilfully, perhaps—not for the mere accident it assuredly was, but for the sly escape of a spontaneous feeling on Billy's part more or less answering to the antipathy on his own. In effect a foolish demonstration, he must have thought, and very harmless, like the futile kick of a heifer, which yet were the heifer a shod stallion would not be so harmless. Even so was it that into the gall of Claggart's envy he infused the vitriol of his contempt. But the incident confirmed to him certain telltale reports purveyed to his ear by "Squeak," one of his more cunning corporals, a grizzled little man, so nicknamed by the sailors on account of his squeaky voice and sharp visage ferreting about the dark corners of the lower decks after interlopers, satirically suggesting to them the idea of a rat in a cellar.

From his chief's employing him as an implicit tool in laying little traps for the worriment of the foretopman—for it was from the master-at-arms that the petty persecutions heretofore adverted to had proceeded—the corporal, having naturally enough concluded that his master could have no love for the sailor, made it his business, faithful understrapper that he was, to foment the ill blood by perverting to his chief certain innocent frolics of the good-natured foretopman, besides inventing for his mouth sundry contumelious epithets he claimed to have overheard him let fall. The master-at-arms never suspected the veracity of these reports, more especially as to the epithets, for he well knew how secretly unpopular may become a master-at-arms, at least a master-at-arms of those days, zealous in his function, and how the bluejackets shoot at him in private their raillery and wit; the nickname by which he goes among them (Jemmy Legs) implying under the form of merriment their cherished disrespect and dislike. But in view of the greediness of hate for pabulum it hardly needed a purveyor to feed Claggart's passion.

An uncommon prudence is habitual with the subtler depravity, for it has everything to hide. And in case of an injury but suspected, its secretiveness voluntarily cuts it off from enlightenment or disillusion; and, not unreluctantly, action is taken upon surmise as upon certainty. And the retaliation is apt to be in monstrous disproportion to the supposed offense; for when in anybody was revenge in its exactions aught else but an inordinate usurer? But how with Claggart's conscience? For though consciences are unlike as foreheads, every intelligence, not excluding the scriptural devils[2] who "believe and tremble," has one. But Claggart's conscience being but the lawyer to his will, made ogres of trifles, probably arguing that the motive imputed to Billy in spilling the soup just when he did, together with the epithets alleged, these, if nothing more, made a strong case against him; nay, justified animosity into a sort of retributive righteousness. The Pharisee[3] is the Guy Fawkes[4] prowling in the hid chambers underlying some natures like Claggart's. And they can really form no conception of an unreciprocated malice. Probably the master-at-arms' clandestine persecution of Billy was started to try the temper of the man; but it had not developed any quality in him that enmity could make official use of or even pervert into plausible self-justification; so that the occurrence at the mess, petty if it were, was a welcome one to that peculiar conscience assigned to be the private mentor of Claggart; and, for the rest, not improbably it put him upon new experiments.

14

Not many days after the last incident narrated, something befell Billy Budd that more graveled him than aught that had previously occurred.

It was a warm night for the latitude; and the foretopman, whose watch at the time was properly below, was dozing on the uppermost deck whither he had ascended from his hot hammock, one of hundreds suspended so closely wedged together over a lower gun deck that there was little or no swing to them. He lay as in the shadow of a hillside, stretched under the lee¹ of the booms, a piled ridge of spare spars amidships between foremast and mainmast among which the ship's largest boat, the launch, was stowed. Alongside of three other slumberers from below, he lay near that end of the booms which approaches the foremast; his station aloft on duty as a foretopman being just over the deck-station of the forecastlemen, entitling him according to usage to make himself more or less at home in that neighborhood.

Presently he was stirred into semiconsciousness by somebody, who must have previously sounded the sleep of the others, touching his shoulder, and then, as the foretopman raised his head, breathing into his ear in a quick whisper, "Slip into the lee forechains, Billy; there is something in the wind. Don't speak. Quick, I will meet you there," and disappearing.

Now Billy, like sundry other essentially good-natured ones, had some of the weaknesses inseparable from essential good nature; and among these was a reluctance, almost an incapacity of plumply saying *no* to an abrupt proposition not obviously absurd on the face of it, nor obviously unfriendly, nor iniquitous. And being of warm blood, he had not the phlegm tacitly to negative any proposition by unresponsive inaction. Like his sense of fear, his apprehension as to aught outside of the honest and natural was seldom very quick. Besides, upon the present occasion, the drowse from his sleep still hung upon him.

However it was, he mechanically rose and, sleepily wondering what could be in the wind, betook himself to the designated place, a narrow platform, one of six, outside of the high bulwarks and screened by the great deadeyes and multiple columned lanyards of the shrouds and backstays;[2] and, in a great warship of that time, of dimensions commensurate to the hull's magnitude; a tarry balcony in short, overhanging the sea, and so secluded that one mariner of the *Bellipotent,* a Nonconformist[3] old tar of a serious turn, made it even in daytime his private oratory.[4]

In this retired nook the stranger soon joined Billy Budd. There was no moon as yet; a haze obscured the starlight. He could not distinctly see the stranger's face. Yet from something in the outline and carriage, Billy took him, and correctly, for one of the afterguard.

"Hist! Billy," said the man, in the same quick cautionary whisper as before. "You were impressed, weren't you? Well, so was I"; and he paused, as to mark the effect. But Billy, not knowing exactly what to make of this, said nothing. Then the other: "We are not the only impressed ones, Billy. There's a gang of us.—Couldn't you—help—at a pinch?"

"What do you mean?" demanded Billy, here thoroughly shaking off his drowse.

"Hist, hist!" the hurried whisper now growing husky. "See here," and the man held up two small objects faintly twinkling in the night-light; "see, they are yours, Billy, if you'll only—"

But Billy broke in, and in his resentful eagerness to deliver himself his vocal infirmity somewhat intruded. "D—d—damme, I don't know what you are d—d—driving at, or what you mean, but you had better g—g—go where you belong!" For the moment the fellow, as con-

Allan Melville, the author's father (shown here in 1820), was the patrician son of a Revolutionary War hero who'd taken part in the Boston Tea Party. He struggled hard to maintain an affluent lifestyle for his family, but his business ventures failed, and he died in disgrace when Herman was only twelve. The large debts he left behind forced Herman and his brother to leave school and go to work. (BERKSHIRE ATHENEUM)

Maria Gansevoort Melville, the author's mother, was born into the old Dutch aristocracy of New York State. A stern Calvinist, she was domineering and strict with her eight children. (BERKSHIRE ATHENEUM)

Herman Melville was born in New York City on August 1, 1819, the third of eight children. He signed on to work on a whaling ship when he was nineteen and later called the four years he spent at sea "my Yale and my Harvard." (BERKSHIRE ATHENEUM)

Gansevoort Melville, Herman's older brother, was the clear favorite of both parents. When Herman was only seven his father wrote to a relative that Herman seemed "very backward in speech and somewhat slower in comprehension . . ." when compared to Gansevoort. Gansevoort died suddenly when he was only thirty, just as his brother's first book, *Typee,* was being published. (BERKSHIRE ATHENEUM)

Elizabeth Shaw married Melville in 1847, after his return from sea. She was the daughter of a former business associate of Melville's father and the best friend of Melville's sister Helen. Her wealthy father was the Chief Justice of the Massachusetts Supreme Court, and the Melville family frequently relied upon his financial resources to get them through hard times. (BERKSHIRE ATHENEUM)

The Melville children, circa 1860 (left to right): Stanwix, Francis, Malcolm and Elizabeth. (BERKSHIRE ATHENEUM)

Melville purchased Arrowhead, a 160-acre farm in western Massachusetts, in 1850, the year he wrote most of *Moby-Dick*. He farmed and wrote there until 1863, when he was forced to take a government job in New York to support his family. Arrowhead remains now as a memorial to Melville. (THE BERKSHIRE COUNTY HISTORICAL SOCIETY)

Nathaniel Hawthorne, the author of *The Scarlet Letter,* wa Melville's neighbor in Massachusetts. Hawthorne was a clos friend and major influence on Melville, especially during th time Melville was working on *Moby-Dick.* (NEW HAMPSHIR HISTORICAL SOCIETY)

Malcolm, Melville's oldest child, was just eighteen when he curled up in his bed at home and fatally shot himself in the head. Twenty years later his brother Stanwix, estranged from his parents for many years, died of tuberculosis at age thirty-five. (BERKSHIRE ATHENEUM)

Melville in 1861. His two early books, *Typee* and *Omoo,* gave him a degree of literary fame, but he later sank into literary obscurity. Sadly neglected by the reading public and the critical establishment, Melville was never able to support his family with the ten works of fiction he published in his lifetime. (BERKSHIRE ATHENEUM)

Maria Gansevoort Melville, the author's mother, at age eighty.
With the exception of the four years he spent at sea as a young
man, Melville lived with his overbearing mother until her death in
1872, at the age of eighty-two. (BERKSHIRE ATHENEUM)

Melville spent nearly twenty years working as a deputy customs inspector for New York Harbor, a lowly, poor paying job. *Billy Budd, Sailor* was written after he retired from the Custom's House and was never published in his lifetime. The manuscript lay concealed in a tin box until it was discovered among his papers by a literary scholar in the 1920s. Since its publication in 1924, *Billy Budd, Sailor* has merited a meaningful place in the history of American literature, and has sparked much critical debate over its motifs. (BERKSHIRE ATHENEUM)

Billy Budd, Sailor—the story of the destruction of a youthful innocent—probably had parallels for Melville to the tragic death of his young son Malcolm. This is a still from the 1962 version of the movie, which starred Terence Stamp in the title role. (MORRIS COLLECTION)

The 1962 adaptation of the film was produced and directed by Peter Ustinov (center), who was also one of its stars. (MORRIS COLLECTION)

ritten by composer Benjamin Britten, the popular operatic rsion of *Billy Budd* was first performed in 1951. This is a oto from the 1998 broadcast of a Metropolitan Opera presen- ion. (WINNIE KLOTZ, COURTESY OF METROPOLITAN OPERA)

A still from the 1998 Metropolitan Opera production of *Billy Budd*. British novelist E. M. Forster wrote the libretto. The continuing interest in *Billy Budd, Sailor* is a testimony to Melville's genius and to the timeless themes he explores in his work. (WINNIE KLOTZ, COURTESY OF METROPOLITAN OPERA)

founded, did not stir; and Billy, springing to his feet, said, "If you d—don't start, I'll t—t—toss you back over the r—rail!" There was no mistaking this, and the mysterious emissary decamped, disappearing in the direction of the mainmast in the shadow of the booms.

"Hallo, what's the matter?" here came growling from a forecastleman awakened from his deck-doze by Billy's raised voice. And as the foretopman reappeared and was recognized by him: "Ah, Beauty, is it you? Well, something must have been the matter, for you st—st—stuttered."

"Oh," rejoined Billy, now mastering the impediment, "I found an afterguardsman in our part of the ship here, and I bid him be off where he belongs."

"And is that all you did about it, Foretopman?" gruffly demanded another, an irascible old fellow of brick-colored visage and hair who was known to his associate forecastlemen as "Red Pepper." "Such sneaks I should like to marry to the gunner's daughter!"—by that expression meaning that he would like to subject them to disciplinary castigation over a gun.

However, Billy's rendering of the matter satisfactorily accounted to these inquirers for the brief commotion, since of all the sections of a ship's company the forecastlemen, veterans for the most part and bigoted in their sea prejudices, are the most jealous in resenting territorial encroachments, especially on the part of any of the afterguard, of whom they have but a sorry opinion—chiefly landsmen, never going aloft except to reef or furl the mainsail, and in no wise competent to handle a marlinspike or turn in a deadeye, say.

15

This incident sorely puzzled Billy Budd. It was an entirely new experience, the first time in his life that he had ever been personally approached in underhand intriguing fashion. Prior to this encounter he had known nothing of the afterguardsman, the two men being stationed wide apart, one forward and aloft during his watch, the other on deck and aft.

What could it mean? And could they really be guineas,[1] those two glittering objects the interloper had held up to his (Billy's) eyes? Where could the fellow get guineas? Why, even spare buttons are not so plentiful at sea. The more he turned the matter over, the more he was nonplussed, and made uneasy and discomfited. In his disgustful recoil from an overture which, though he but ill comprehended, he instinctively knew must involve evil of some sort, Billy Budd was like a young horse fresh from the pasture suddenly inhaling a vile whiff from some chemical factory, and by repeated snortings trying to get it out of his nostrils and lungs. This frame of mind barred all desire of holding further parley with the fellow, even were it but for the purpose of gaining some enlightenment as to his design in approaching him. And yet he was not without natural curiosity to see how such a visitor in the dark would look in broad day.

He espied him the following afternoon in his first dogwatch below, one of the smokers on that forward part of the upper gun deck allotted to the pipe. He recognized him by his general cut and build more than by his round freckled face and glassy eyes of pale blue, veiled with lashes all but white. And yet Billy was a bit uncertain whether indeed it were he—yonder chap about his own age chatting and laughing in freehearted way, leaning against a gun; a genial young fellow enough to look at, and something of a rattlebrain, to all appearance. Rather chubby too for a sailor, even an afterguardsman. In short, the last man in the world, one would think, to be overburdened with thoughts, especially those perilous thoughts that must needs belong to a conspirator in any serious project, or even to the underling of such a conspirator.

Although Billy was not aware of it, the fellow, with a sidelong watchful glance, had perceived Billy first, and then noting that Billy was looking at him, thereupon nodded a familiar sort of friendly recognition as to an old acquaintance, without interrupting the talk he was engaged in with the group of smokers. A day or two afterwards, chancing in the evening promenade on a gun deck to pass Billy, he offered a flying word of good-fellowship, as it were, which by its unexpectedness, and equivocalness under the circumstances, so embarrassed Billy that he knew not how to respond to it, and let it go unnoticed.

Billy was now left more at a loss than before. The ineffectual speculations into which he was led were so disturbingly alien to him that he did his best to smother them. It never entered his mind that here was a matter which, from its extreme questionableness, it was his duty as a loyal bluejacket to report in the proper quarter. And, probably, had such a step been suggested to him, he would have been deterred from taking it by the thought, one of novice magnanimity, that it would savor overmuch of the dirty work of a telltale. He kept the thing to himself. Yet upon one occasion he could not forbear a little disburdening himself to the old Dansker, tempted thereto perhaps by the influence of a balmy night when the ship lay becalmed; the twain, silent for the most part, sitting together on deck, their heads propped against the bulwarks. But it was only a partial and anonymous account that Billy gave, the unfounded scruples above referred to preventing full disclosure to anybody. Upon hearing Billy's version, the sage Dansker seemed to divine more than he was told; and after a little meditation, during which his wrinkles were pursed as into a point, quite effacing for the time that quizzing expression his face sometimes wore: "Didn't I say so, Baby Budd?"

"Say what?" demanded Billy.

"Why, *Jemmy Legs* is *down* on you."

"And what," rejoined Billy in amazement, "has *Jemmy Legs* to do with that cracked afterguardsman?"

"Ho, it was an afterguardsman, then. A cat's-paw, a cat's-paw!" And with that exclamation, whether it had reference to a light puff of air just then coming over the calm sea, or a subtler relation to the afterguardsman, there is no telling, the old Merlin gave a twisting wrench with his black teeth at his plug of tobacco, vouchsafing no reply to Billy's impetuous question, though now repeated, for it was his wont to relapse into grim silence when interrogated in skeptical sort as to any of his sententious oracles, not always very clear ones, rather partaking of that obscurity which invests most Delphic[2] deliverances from any quarter.

Long experience had very likely brought this old man to that bitter prudence which never interferes in aught and never gives advice.

16

Yes, despite the Dansker's pithy insistence as to the master-at-arms being at the bottom of these strange experiences of Billy on board the *Bellipotent,* the young sailor was ready to ascribe them to almost anybody but the man who, to use Billy's own expression, "always had a pleasant word for him." This is to be wondered at. Yet not so much to be wondered at. In certain matters, some sailors even in mature life remain unsophisticated enough. But a young seafarer of the disposition of our athletic foretopman is much of a child-man. And yet a child's utter innocence is but its blank ignorance, and the innocence more or less wanes as intelligence waxes. But in Billy Budd intelligence, such as it was, had advanced while yet his simplemindedness remained for the most part unaffected. Experience is a teacher indeed; yet did Billy's years make his experience small. Besides, he had none of that intuitive knowledge of the bad which in natures not good or incompletely so foreruns experience, and therefore may pertain, as in some instances it too clearly does pertain, even to youth.

And what could Billy know of man except of man as a mere sailor? And the old-fashioned sailor, the veritable man before the mast, the sailor from boyhood up, he, though indeed of the same species as a landsman, is in some respects singularly distinct from him. The sailor is frankness, the landsman is finesse. Life is not a game with the sailor, demanding the long head—no intricate game of chess where few moves are made in straightforwardness and ends are attained by indirection, an oblique, tedious, barren game hardly worth that poor candle burnt out in playing it.

Yes, as a class, sailors are in character a juvenile race. Even their deviations are marked by juvenility, this more especially holding true with the sailors of Billy's time. Then too, certain things which apply to all sailors do more pointedly operate here and there upon the junior one. Every sailor, too, is accustomed to obey orders without debating them; his life afloat is externally ruled for him; he is not brought into that promiscuous commerce with mankind where unobstructed free agency on equal terms—equal superficially, at least—soon teaches one that unless upon occasion he exercise a distrust keen in proportion to the fairness of the appearance, some foul turn may be served him. A ruled undemonstrative distrustfulness is so habitual, not with businessmen so much as with men who know their kind in less shallow relations than business, namely, certain men of the world, that they come at last to employ it all but unconsciously; and some of them would very likely feel real surprise at being charged with it as one of their general characteristics.

17

But after the little matter at the mess Billy Budd no more found himself in strange trouble at times about his hammock or his clothes bag or what not. As to that smile that occasionally sunned him, and the pleasant passing word, these were, if not more frequent, yet if anything more pronounced than before.

But for all that, there were certain other demonstrations now. When Claggart's unobserved glance happened to light on belted Billy rolling along the upper gun deck in the leisure of the second dogwatch, exchanging passing broadsides of fun with other young promenaders in the crowd, that glance would follow the cheerful sea Hyperion[1] with a settled meditative and melancholy expression, his eyes strangely suffused with incipient feverish tears. Then would Claggart look like the man of sorrows.[2] Yes, and sometimes the melancholy expression would have in it a touch of soft yearning, as if Claggart could even have loved Billy but for fate and ban. But this was an evanescence, and quickly repented of, as it were, by an immitigable look, pinching and shriveling the visage into the momentary semblance of a wrinkled walnut. But sometimes catching sight in advance of the foretopman coming in his direction, he would, upon their nearing, step aside a little to let him pass, dwelling upon Billy for the moment with the glittering dental satire of a Guise.[3] But upon any abrupt unforeseen encounter a red light would flash forth from his eye like a spark from an anvil in a dusk smithy. That quick, fierce light was a strange one, darted from orbs which in repose were of a color nearest approaching a deeper violet, the softest of shades.

Though some of these caprices of the pit could not but be observed by their object, yet were they beyond the construing of such a nature. And the thews[4] of Billy were hardly compatible with that sort of sensitive spiritual organization which in some cases instinctively conveys to ignorant innocence an admonition of the proximity of the malign. He thought the master-at-arms acted in a manner rather queer at times. That was all. But the occasional frank air and pleasant word went for what they purported to be, the young sailor never having heard as yet of the "too fair-spoken man."

Had the foretopman been conscious of having done or said anything to provoke the ill will of the official, it would have been different with him, and his sight might have been purged if not sharpened. As it was, innocence was his blinder.

So was it with him in yet another matter. Two minor officers, the armorer and captain of the hold, with whom he had never exchanged a word, his position in the ship not bringing him into contact with them, these men now for the first began to cast upon Billy, when they chanced to encounter him, that peculiar glance which evidences that the man from whom it comes has been some way tampered with, and to the prejudice of him upon whom the glance lights. Never did it occur to Billy as a thing to be noted or a thing suspicious, though he well knew the fact, that the armorer and captain of the hold, with the ship's yeoman, apothecary, and others of that grade, were by naval usage messmates of the master-at-arms, men with ears convenient to his confidential tongue.

But the general popularity that came from our Handsome Sailor's manly forwardness upon occasion and irresistible good nature, indicating no mental superiority tending to excite an invidious feeling, this good will on the part of most of his shipmates made him the less to concern himself about such mute aspects toward him as those whereto allusion has just been made, aspects he could not so fathom as to infer their whole import.

As to the afterguardsman, though Billy for reasons already given necessarily saw little of him, yet when the two did happen to meet, invariably came the fellow's offhand cheerful recognition, sometimes accompanied by a passing pleasant word or two. Whatever that equivocal young person's original design may really have been, or the design of which he might have been the deputy, certain it was from his manner upon these occasions that he had wholly dropped it.

It was as if his precocity of crookedness (and every vulgar villain is precocious) had for once deceived him, and the man he had sought to entrap as a simpleton had through his very simplicity ignominiously baffled him.

But shrewd ones may opine that it was hardly possible for Billy to refrain from going up to the afterguardsman and bluntly demanding to know his purpose in the initial interview so abruptly closed in the forechains. Shrewd ones may also think it but natural in Billy to set about sounding some of the other impressed men of the ship in order to discover what basis, if any, there was for the emissary's obscure suggestions as to plotting disaffection aboard. Yes, shrewd ones may so think. But something more, or rather something else than mere shrewdness is perhaps needful for the due understanding of such a character as Billy Budd's.

As to Claggart, the monomania in the man—if that

indeed it were—as involuntarily disclosed by starts in the manifestations detailed, yet in general covered over by his self-contained and rational demeanor; this, like a subterranean fire, was eating its way deeper and deeper in him. Something decisive must come of it.

18

After the mysterious interview in the forechains, the one so abruptly ended there by Billy, nothing especially germane to the story occurred until the events now about to be narrated.

Elsewhere it has been said that in the lack of frigates (of course better sailers than line-of-battle ships) in the English squadron up the Straits[1] at that period, the *Bellipotent 74* was occasionally employed not only as an available substitute for a scout, but at times on detached service of more important kind. This was not alone because of her sailing qualities, not common in a ship of her rate, but quite as much, probably, that the character of her commander, it was thought, specially adapted him for any duty where under unforeseen difficulties a prompt initiative might have to be taken in some matter demanding knowledge and ability in addition to those qualities implied in good seamanship. It was on an expedition of the latter sort, a somewhat distant one, and when the *Bellipotent* was almost at her furthest remove from the fleet, that in the latter part of an afternoon watch she unexpectedly came in sight of a ship of the enemy. It proved to be a frigate. The latter, perceiving through the glass that the weight of men and metal would be heavily against her, invoking her light heels crowded sail to get away. After a chase urged almost against hope and lasting until about the middle of the first dogwatch, she signally succeeded in effecting her escape.

Not long after the pursuit had been given up, and ere the excitement incident thereto had altogether waned away, the master-at-arms, ascending from his cavernous sphere, made his appearance cap in hand by the mainmast respectfully waiting the notice of Captain Vere, then solitary walking the weather side of the quarter-deck, doubtless somewhat chafed at the failure of the pursuit. The spot where Claggart stood was the place allotted to men of lesser grades seeking some more particular interview either with the officer of the deck or the captain himself. But from the latter it was not often that a sailor or petty officer of those days would seek a hearing; only some exceptional cause would, according to established custom, have warranted that.

Presently, just as the commander, absorbed in his reflections, was on the point of turning aft in his promenade, he became sensible of Claggart's presence, and saw the doffed cap held in deferential expectancy. Here be it said that Captain Vere's personal knowledge of this petty officer had only begun at the time of the ship's last sailing from home, Claggart then for the first, in transfer from a ship detained for repairs, supplying on board the *Bellipotent* the place of a previous master-at-arms disabled and ashore.

No sooner did the commander observe who it was that now deferentially stood awaiting his notice than a peculiar expression came over him. It was not unlike that which uncontrollably will flit across the countenance of one at unawares encountering a person who, though known to him indeed, has hardly been long enough known for thorough knowledge, but something in whose aspect nevertheless now for the first provokes a vaguely repellent distaste. But coming to a stand and resuming much of his wonted official manner, save that a sort of impatience lurked in the intonation of the opening word, he said "Well? What is it, Master-at-arms?"

With the air of a subordinate grieved at the necessity of being a messenger of ill tidings, and while conscientiously determined to be frank yet equally resolved upon shunning overstatement, Claggart at this invitation, or rather summons to disburden, spoke up. What he said, conveyed in the language of no uneducated man, was to the effect following, if not altogether in these words, namely, that during the chase and preparations for the possible encounter he had seen enough to convince him that at least one sailor aboard was a dangerous character in a ship mustering some who not only had taken a guilty part in the late serious troubles, but others also who, like the man in question, had entered His Majesty's service under another form than enlistment.

At this point Captain Vere with some impatience interrupted him: "Be direct, man; say *impressed men.*"

Claggart made a gesture of subservience, and proceeded. Quite lately he (Claggart) had begun to suspect that on the gun decks some sort of movement prompted by the sailor in question was covertly going on, but he had not thought himself warranted in reporting the suspicion so long as it remained indistinct. But from what he had that afternoon observed in the man referred to, the suspicion of something clandestine going on had advanced to a point less removed from certainty. He deeply felt, he added, the serious responsibility assumed in making a report involving such possible consequences to the individual mainly concerned, besides tending to augment those natural anxieties which every naval commander must feel in view of extraordinary outbreaks so recent as those which, he sorrowfully said it, it needed not to name.

Now at the first broaching of the matter Captain Vere, taken by surprise, could not wholly dissemble his disquietude. But as Claggart went on, the former's aspect changed into restiveness under something in the testifier's manner in giving his testimony. However, he refrained from interrupting him. And Claggart, continuing, concluded with this: "God forbid, your honor, that the *Bellipotent*'s should be the experience of the ———"

"Never mind that!" here peremptorily broke in the superior, his face altering with anger, instinctively divining the ship that the other was about to name, one in which the Nore Mutiny had assumed a singularly tragical character that for a time jeopardized the life of its commander. Under the circumstances he was indignant at the purposed allusion. When the commissioned officers themselves were on all occasions very heedful how they referred to the recent events in the fleet, for a petty officer unnecessarily to allude to them in the presence of his captain, this struck him as a most immodest presumption. Besides, to his quick sense of self-respect it even looked under the circumstances something like an attempt to alarm him. Nor at first was he without some surprise that one who so far as he had hitherto come under his notice had shown considerable tact in his function should in this particular evince such lack of it.

But these thoughts and kindred dubious ones flitting across his mind were suddenly replaced by an intuitional surmise which, though as yet obscure in form, served practically to affect his reception of the ill tidings. Certain it is that, long versed in everything pertaining to the complicated gun-deck life, which like every other form of life has its secret mines and dubious side, the side popularly disclaimed, Captain Vere did not permit himself to be unduly disturbed by the general tenor of his subordinate's report.

Furthermore, if in view of recent events prompt action should be taken at the first palpable sign of recurring insubordination, for all that, not judicious would it be, he thought, to keep the idea of lingering disaffection alive by undue forwardness in crediting an informer, even if his own subordinate and charged among other things with police surveillance of the crew. This feeling would not perhaps have so prevailed with him were it not that upon a prior occasion the patriotic zeal officially evinced by Claggart had somewhat irritated him as appearing rather supersensible and strained. Furthermore, something even in the official's self-possessed and somewhat ostentatious manner in making his specifications strangely reminded him of a bandsman,[2] a perjurous witness in a capital case before a court-martial ashore of which when a lieutenant he (Captain Vere) had been a member.

Now the peremptory check given to Claggart in the matter of the arrested allusion was quickly followed up by this: "You say that there is at least one dangerous man aboard. Name him."

"William Budd, a foretopman, your honor."

"William Budd!" repeated Captain Vere with unfeigned astonishment. "And mean you the man that Lieutenant

Ratcliffe took from the merchantman not very long ago, the young fellow who seems to be so popular with the men—Billy, the Handsome Sailor, as they call him?"

"The same, your honor; but for all his youth and good looks, a deep one. Not for nothing does he insinuate himself into the good will of his shipmates, since at the least they will at a pinch say—all hands will—a good word for him, and at all hazards. Did Lieutenant Ratcliffe happen to tell your honor of that adroit fling of Budd's, jumping up in the cutter's bow under the merchantman's stern when he was being taken off? It is even masked by that sort of good-humored air that at heart he resents his impressment. You have but noted his fair cheek. A mantrap may be under the ruddy-tipped daisies."

Now the Handsome Sailor as a signal figure among the crew had naturally enough attracted the captain's attention from the first. Though in general not very demonstrative to his officers, he had congratulated Lieutenant Ratcliffe upon his good fortune in lighting on such a fine specimen of the *genus homo,*[3] who in the nude might have posed for a statue of young Adam before the Fall. As to Billy's adieu to the ship *Rights-of-Man,* which the boarding lieutenant had indeed reported to him, but, in a deferential way, more as a good story than aught else, Captain Vere, though mistakenly understanding it as a satiric sally, had but thought so much the better of the impressed man for it; as a military sailor, admiring the spirit that could take an arbitrary enlistment so merrily and sensibly. The foretopman's conduct, too, so far as it had fallen under the captain's notice, had confirmed the first happy augury, while the new recruit's qualities as a "sailor-man" seemed to be such that he had thought of recommending him to the executive officer for promotion to a place that would more frequently bring him under his own observation, namely, the captaincy of the mizzentop,[4] replacing there in the starboard watch a man not so young whom partly for that reason he deemed less fitted for the post. Be it parenthesized here that since the mizzentopmen have not to handle such breadths of heavy canvas as the lower sails on the mainmast and foremast, a young man if of the right stuff not only seems best adapted to duty there, but in fact is generally selected for the captaincy of that top, and the company under him are light hands and often but striplings. In sum, Captain Vere had from the beginning deemed Billy Budd to be what in the naval parlance of the time was called a "King's bargain": that is to say, for His Britannic Majesty's navy a capital investment at small outlay or none at all.

After a brief pause, during which the reminiscences above mentioned passed vividly through his mind and he weighed the import of Claggart's last suggestion conveyed in the phrase "mantrap under the daisies," and the more he weighed it the less reliance he felt in the informer's good faith, suddenly he turned upon him and in a low voice demanded: "Do you come to me, Master-at-arms, with so foggy a tale? As to Budd, cite me an act or spoken word of his confirmatory of what you in general charge against him. Stay," drawing nearer to him; "heed what you speak. Just now, and in a case like this, there is a yardarm-end[5] for the false witness."

"Ah, your honor!" sighed Claggart, mildly shaking his shapely head as in sad deprecation of such unmerited severity of tone. Then, bridling—erecting himself as in virtuous self-assertion—he circumstantially alleged certain words and acts which collectively, if credited, led to presumptions mortally inculpating Budd. And for some of these averments, he added, substantiating proof was not far.

With gray eyes impatient and distrustful essaying to fathom to the bottom Claggart's calm violet ones, Captain Vere again heard him out; then for the moment stood ruminating. The mood he evinced, Claggart—himself for the time liberated from the other's scrutiny—steadily regarded with a look difficult to render: a look curious of the operation of his tactics, a look such as might have been that of the spokesman of the envious children of Jacob deceptively imposing upon the troubled patriarch the blood-dyed coat of young Joseph.[6]

Though something exceptional in the moral quality of Captain Vere made him, in earnest encounter with a fellow man, a veritable touchstone of that man's essential nature, yet now as to Claggart and what was really going on in him his feeling partook less of intuitional conviction than of strong suspicion clogged by strange dubieties. The perplexity he evinced proceeded less from aught touching the man informed against—as Claggart doubtless opined—than from considerations how best to act in regard to the informer. At first, indeed, he was naturally for summoning that substantiation of his allegations which Claggart said was at hand. But such a proceeding would result in the matter at once getting abroad, which in the present stage of it, he thought, might undesirably affect the ship's company. If Claggart was a false witness—that closed the affair. And therefore, before trying the accusation, he would first practically test the accuser; and he thought this could be done in a quiet, undemonstrative way.

The measure he determined upon involved a shifting of the scene, a transfer to a place less exposed to observation than the broad quarter-deck. For although the few gunroom officers there at the time had, in due observance of naval etiquette, withdrawn to leeward the moment Captain Vere had begun his promenade on the deck's weather side; and though during the colloquy with Claggart they of course ventured not to diminish the distance; and though throughout the interview Captain Vere's voice was far from high, and Claggart's silvery and low; and the wind in the cordage and the wash of the sea helped the more to put them beyond earshot; nevertheless, the interview's continuance already had attracted observation from some topmen aloft and other sailors in the waist or further forward.

Having determined upon his measures, Captain Vere forthwith took action. Abruptly turning to Claggart, he asked, "Master-at-arms, is it now Budd's watch aloft?"

"No, your honor."

Whereupon, "Mr. Wilkes!" summoning the nearest midshipman. "Tell Albert to come to me." Albert was the captain's hammock-boy, a sort of sea valet in whose discretion and fidelity his master had much confidence. The lad appeared.

"You know Budd, the foretopman?"

"I do, sir."

"Go find him. It is his watch off. Manage to tell him out

of earshot that he is wanted aft. Contrive it that he speaks to nobody. Keep him in talk yourself. And not till you get well aft here, not till then let him know that the place where he is wanted is my cabin. You understand. Go.— Master-at-arms, show yourself on the decks below, and when you think it time for Albert to be coming with his man, stand by quietly to follow the sailor in."

19

Now when the foretopman found himself in the cabin, closeted there, as it were, with the captain and Claggart, he was surprised enough. But it was a surprise unaccompanied by apprehension or distrust. To an immature nature essentially honest and humane, forewarning intimations of subtler danger from one's kind come tardily if at all. The only thing that took shape in the young sailor's mind was this: Yes, the captain, I have always thought, looks kindly upon me. Wonder if he's going to make me his coxswain. I should like that. And may be now he is going to ask the master-at-arms about me.

"Shut the door there, sentry," said the commander; "stand without, and let nobody come in.—Now, Master-at-arms, tell this man to his face what you told of him to me," and stood prepared to scrutinize the mutually confronting visages.

With the measured step and calm collected air of an asylum physician approaching in the public hall some patient beginning to show indications of a coming paroxysm, Claggart deliberately advanced within short range of Billy and, mesmerically looking him in the eye, briefly recapitulated the accusation.

Not at first did Billy take it in. When he did, the rose-tan of his cheek looked struck as by white leprosy. He stood like one impaled and gagged. Meanwhile the accuser's eyes, removing not as yet from the blue dilated ones, underwent a phenomenal change, their wonted rich violet color blurring into a muddy purple. Those lights of human intelligence, losing human expression, were gelidly protruding like the alien eyes of certain uncatalogued creatures of the deep. The first mesmeristic glance was one of serpent fascination; the last was as the paralyzing lurch of the torpedo fish.[1]

"Speak, man!" said Captain Vere to the transfixed one, struck by his aspect even more than by Claggart's. "Speak! Defend yourself!" Which appeal caused but a strange dumb gesturing and gurgling in Billy; amazement at such an accusation so suddenly sprung on inexperienced nonage; this, and, it may be, horror of the accuser's eyes, serving to bring out his lurking defect and in this instance for the time intensifying it into a convulsed tongue-tie; while the intent head and entire form straining forward in an agony of ineffectual eagerness to obey the injunction to speak and defend himself, gave an expression to the face like that of a condemned vestal priestess in the moment of being buried alive, and in the first struggle against suffocation.[2]

Though at the time Captain Vere was quite ignorant of Billy's liability to vocal impediment, he now immediately divined it, since vividly Billy's aspect recalled to him that of a bright young schoolmate of his whom he had once seen struck by much the same startling impotence in the act of eagerly rising in the class to be foremost in response to a testing question put to it by the master. Going close up to the young sailor, and laying a soothing hand on his shoulder, he said, "There is no hurry, my boy. Take your time, take your time." Contrary to the effect intended, these words so fatherly in tone, doubtless touching Billy's heart to the quick, prompted yet more violent efforts at utterance—efforts soon ending for the time in confirming the paralysis, and bringing to his face an expression which was as a crucifixion to behold. The next instant, quick as the flame from a discharged cannon at night, his right arm shot out, and Claggart dropped to the deck. Whether intentionally or but owing to the young athlete's superior height, the blow had taken effect full upon the forehead, so shapely and intellectual-looking a feature in the master-at-arms; so that the body fell over lengthwise, like a heavy plank tilted from erectness. A gasp or two, and he lay motionless.

"Fated boy," breathed Captain Vere in tone so low as to be almost a whisper, "what have you done! But here, help me."

The twain raised the felled one from the loins up into a sitting position. The spare form flexibly acquiesced, but inertly. It was like handling a dead snake. They lowered it back. Regaining erectness, Captain Vere with one hand covering his face stood to all appearance as impassive as the object at his feet. Was he absorbed in taking in all the bearings of the event and what was best not only now at once to be done, but also in the sequel? Slowly he uncovered his face; and the effect was as if the moon emerging from eclipse should reappear with quite another aspect than that which had gone into hiding. The father in him, manifested towards Billy thus far in the scene, was replaced by the military disciplinarian. In his official tone he bade the foretopman retire to a stateroom aft (pointing it out), and there remain till thence summoned. This order Billy in silence mechanically obeyed. Then going to the cabin door where it opened on the quarter-deck, Captain Vere said to the sentry without, "Tell somebody to send Albert here." When the lad appeared, his master so contrived it that he should not catch sight of the prone one. "Albert," he said to him, "tell the surgeon I wish to see him. You need not come back till called."

When the surgeon entered—a self-poised character of that grave sense and experience that hardly anything could take him aback—Captain Vere advanced to meet him, thus unconsciously intercepting his view of Claggart, and, interrupting the other's wonted ceremonious salutation, said, "Nay. Tell me how it is with yonder man," directing his attention to the prostrate one.

The surgeon looked, and for all his self-command somewhat started at the abrupt revelation. On Claggart's always pallid complexion, thick black blood was now oozing from nostril and ear. To the gazer's professional eye it was unmistakably no living man that he saw.

"Is it so, then?" said Captain Vere, intently watching him. "I thought it. But verify it." Whereupon the customary tests confirmed the surgeon's first glance, who now, looking up in unfeigned concern, cast a look of intense inquisitiveness upon his superior. But Captain Vere, with one hand to his brow, was standing motionless. Suddenly, catching the surgeon's arm convulsively, he exclaimed, pointing down to the body, "It is the divine judgment on Ananias![3] Look!"

Disturbed by the excited manner he had never before observed in the *Bellipotent*'s captain, and as yet wholly ignorant of the affair, the prudent surgeon nevertheless held his peace, only again looking an earnest interrogatory as to what it was that had resulted in such a tragedy.

But Captain Vere was now again motionless, standing absorbed in thought. Again starting, he vehemently exclaimed, "Struck dead by an angel of God! Yet the angel must hang!"[4]

At these passionate interjections, mere incoherences to the listener as yet unapprised of the antecedents, the surgeon was profoundly discomposed. But now, as recollecting himself, Captain Vere in less passionate tone briefly related the circumstances leading up to the event. "But come; we must dispatch," he added. "Help me to remove him" (meaning the body) "to yonder compartment," designating one opposite that where the foretopman remained immured. Anew disturbed by a request that, as implying a desire for secrecy, seemed unaccountably strange to him, there was nothing for the subordinate to do but comply.

"Go now," said Captain Vere with something of his wonted manner. "Go now. I presently shall call a drumhead court.[5] Tell the lieutenants what has happened, and tell Mr. Mordant" (meaning the captain of marines[6]), "and charge them to keep the matter to themselves."

20

Full of disquietude and misgiving, the surgeon left the cabin. Was Captain Vere suddenly affected in his mind, or was it but a transient excitement, brought about by so strange and extraordinary a tragedy? As to the drumhead court, it struck the surgeon as impolitic, if nothing more.

The thing to do, he thought, was to place Billy Budd in confinement, and in a way dictated by usage, and postpone further action in so extraordinary a case to such time as they should rejoin the squadron, and then refer it to the admiral. He recalled the unwonted agitation of Captain Vere and his excited exclamations, so at variance with his normal manner. Was he unhinged?

But assuming that he is, it is not so susceptible of proof. What then can the surgeon do? No more trying situation is conceivable than that of an officer subordinate under a captain whom he suspects to be not mad, indeed, but yet not quite unaffected in his intellects. To argue his order to him would be insolence. To resist him would be mutiny.

In obedience to Captain Vere, he communicated what had happened to the lieutenants and captain of marines, saying nothing as to the captain's state. They fully shared his own surprise and concern. Like him too, they seemed to think that such a matter should be referred to the admiral.

21

Who in the rainbow can draw the line where the violet tint ends and the orange tint begins? Distinctly we see the difference of the colors, but where exactly does the one first blendingly enter into the other? So with sanity and insanity. In pronounced cases there is no question about them. But in some supposed cases, in various degrees supposedly less pronounced, to draw the exact line of demarcation few will undertake, though for a fee becoming considerate some professional experts will. There is nothing namable but that some men will, or undertake to, do it for pay.

Whether Captain Vere, as the surgeon professionally and privately surmised, was really the sudden victim of any degree of aberration, every one must determine for himself by such light as this narrative may afford.

That the unhappy event which has been narrated could not have happened at a worse juncture was but too true.

For it was close on the heel of the suppressed insurrections, an aftertime very critical to naval authority, demanding from every English sea commander two qualities not readily interfusable—prudence and rigor. Moreover, there was something crucial in the case.

In the jugglery of circumstances preceding and attending the event on board the *Bellipotent,* and in the light of that martial code whereby it was formally to be judged, innocence and guilt personified in Claggart and Budd in effect changed places. In a legal view the apparent victim of the tragedy was he who had sought to victimize a man blameless; and the indisputable deed of the latter, navally regarded, constituted the most heinous of military crimes. Yet more. The essential right and wrong involved in the matter, the clearer that might be, so much the worse for the responsibility of a loyal sea commander, inasmuch as he was not authorized to determine the matter on that primitive basis.

Small wonder then that the *Bellipotent*'s captain, though in general a man of rapid decision, felt that circumspectness not less than promptitude was necessary. Until he could decide upon his course, and in each detail; and not only so, but until the concluding measure was upon the point of being enacted, he deemed it advisable, in view of all the circumstances, to guard as much as possible against publicity. Here he may or may not have erred. Certain it is, however, that subsequently in the confidential talk of more than one or two gun rooms and cabins he was not a little criticized by some officers, a fact imputed by his friends and vehemently by his cousin Jack Denton to professional jealousy of Starry Vere. Some imaginative ground for invidious comment there was. The maintenance of secrecy in the matter, the confining all knowledge of it for a time to the place where the homicide occurred, the quarter-deck cabin; in these particulars lurked some resemblance to the policy adopted in those tragedies of the palace which have occurred more than once in the capital founded by Peter the Barbarian.[1]

The case indeed was such that fain would the *Bellipotent*'s captain have deferred taking any action whatever respecting it further than to keep the foretopman a close prisoner till the ship rejoined the squadron and then submitting the matter to the judgment of his admiral.

But a true military officer is in one particular like a true monk. Not with more of self-abnegation will the latter keep his vows of monastic obedience than the former his vows of allegiance to martial duty.

Feeling that unless quick action was taken on it, the deed of the foretopman, so soon as it should be known on the gun decks, would tend to awaken any slumbering embers of the Nore among the crew, a sense of the urgency of the case overruled in Captain Vere every other consideration. But though a conscientious disciplinarian, he was no lover of authority for mere authority's sake. Very far was he from embracing opportunities for monopolizing to himself the perils of moral responsibility, none at least that could properly be referred to an official superior or shared with him by his official equals or even subordinates. So thinking, he was glad it would not be at variance with usage to turn the matter over to a summary court of his own officers, reserving to himself, as the one on whom the ultimate accountability would rest, the right of maintaining a supervision of it, or formally or informally interposing at need. Accordingly a drumhead court was summarily convened, he electing the individuals composing it: the first lieutenant, the captain of marines, and the sailing master.[2]

In associating an officer of marines with the sea lieutenant and the sailing master in a case having to do with a sailor, the commander perhaps deviated from general custom. He was prompted thereto by the circumstance that he took that soldier to be a judicious person, thoughtful, and not altogether incapable of grappling with a difficult case unprecedented in his prior experience. Yet even as to him he was not without some latent misgiving, for withal he was an extremely good-natured man, an enjoyer of his dinner, a sound sleeper, and inclined to obesity—a man who though he would always maintain his manhood in battle might not prove altogether reliable in a moral dilemma involving aught of the tragic. As to the first lieutenant and the sailing master, Captain Vere could not but be aware that though honest natures, of approved gallantry upon occasion, their intelligence was mostly confined to the matter of active seamanship and the fighting demands of their profession.

The court was held in the same cabin where the unfortunate affair had taken place. This cabin, the commander's, embraced the entire area under the poop deck. Aft, and on either side, was a small stateroom, the one now temporarily a jail and the other a dead-house, and a yet smaller compartment, leaving a space between expanding forward into a goodly oblong of length coinciding with the ship's beam.[3] A skylight of moderate dimension was overhead, and at each end of the oblong space were two sashed porthole windows easily convertible back into embrasures for short carronades.[4]

All being quickly in readiness, Billy Budd was arraigned, Captain Vere necessarily appearing as the sole witness in the case, and as such temporarily sinking his rank, though singularly maintaining it in a matter apparently trivial, namely, that he testified from the ship's weather side, with that object having caused the court to sit on the lee side.[5] Concisely he narrated all that had led up to the catastrophe, omitting nothing in Claggart's accusation and deposing as to the manner in which the prisoner had received it. At this testimony the three officers glanced with no little surprise at Billy Budd, the last man they would have suspected either of the mutinous design alleged by Claggart or the undeniable deed he himself had done. The first lieutenant, taking judicial primacy and turning toward the prisoner, said, "Captain Vere has spoken. Is it or is it not as Captain Vere says?"

In response came syllables not so much impeded in the utterance as might have been anticipated. They were these: "Captain Vere tells the truth. It is just as Captain Vere says, but it is not as the master-at-arms said. I have eaten the King's bread and I am true to the King."

"I believe you, my man," said the witness, his voice indicating a suppressed emotion not otherwise betrayed.

"God will bless you for that, your honor!" not without

stammering said Billy, and all but broke down. But immediately he was recalled to self-control by another question, to which with the same emotional difficulty of utterance he said, "No, there was no malice between us. I never bore malice against the master-at-arms. I am sorry that he is dead. I did not mean to kill him. Could I have used my tongue I would not have struck him. But he foully lied to my face and in presence of my captain, and I had to say something, and I could only say it with a blow, God help me!"

In the impulsive aboveboard manner of the frank one the court saw confirmed all that was implied in words that just previously had perplexed them, coming as they did from the testifier to the tragedy and promptly following Billy's impassioned disclaimer of mutinous intent—Captain Vere's words, "I believe you, my man."

Next it was asked of him whether he knew of or suspected aught savoring of incipient trouble (meaning mutiny, though the explicit term was avoided) going on in any section of the ship's company.

The reply lingered. This was naturally imputed by the court to the same vocal embarrassment which had retarded or obstructed previous answers. But in main it was otherwise here, the question immediately recalling to Billy's mind the interview with the afterguardsman in the forechains. But an innate repugnance to playing a part at all approaching that of an informer against one's own shipmates—the same erring sense of uninstructed honor which had stood in the way of his reporting the matter at the time, though as a loyal man-of-war's man it was incumbent on him, and failure so to do, if charged against him and proven, would have subjected him to the heaviest of penalties; this, with the blind feeling now his that nothing really was being hatched, prevailed with him. When the answer came it was a negative.

"One question more," said the officer of marines, now first speaking and with a troubled earnestness. "You tell us that what the master-at-arms said against you was a lie. Now why should he have so lied, so maliciously lied, since you declare there was no malice between you?"

At that question, unintentionally touching on a spiritual sphere wholly obscure to Billy's thoughts, he was nonplussed, evincing a confusion indeed that some observers, such as can readily be imagined, would have construed into involuntary evidence of hidden guilt. Nevertheless, he strove some way to answer, but all at once relinquished the vain endeavor, at the same time turning an appealing glance towards Captain Vere as deeming him his best helper and friend. Captain Vere, who had been seated for a time, rose to his feet, addressing the interrogator. "The question you put to him comes naturally enough. But how can he rightly answer it?—or anybody else, unless indeed it be he who lies within there," designating the compartment where lay the corpse. "But the prone one there will not rise to our summons. In effect, though, as it seems to me, the point you make is hardly material. Quite aside from any conceivable motive actuating the master-at-arms, and irrespective of the provocation to the blow, a martial court must needs in the present case confine its attention to the blow's consequence, which consequence justly is to be deemed not otherwise than as the striker's deed."

This utterance, the full significance of which it was not at all likely that Billy took in, nevertheless caused him to turn a wistful interrogative look toward the speaker, a look in its dumb expressiveness not unlike that which a dog of generous breed might turn upon his master, seeking in his face some elucidation of a previous gesture ambiguous to the canine intelligence. Nor was the same utterance without marked effect upon the three officers, more especially the soldier. Couched in it seemed to them a meaning unanticipated, involving a prejudgment on the speaker's part. It served to augment a mental disturbance previously evident enough.

The soldier once more spoke, in a tone of suggestive dubiety addressing at once his associates and Captain Vere: "Nobody is present—none of the ship's company, I mean—who might shed lateral light, if any is to be had, upon what remains mysterious in this matter."

"That is thoughtfully put," said Captain Vere; "I see

your drift. Ay, there is a mystery; but, to use a scriptural phrase, it is a 'mystery of iniquity,'[6] a matter for psychologic theologians to discuss. But what has a military court to do with it? Not to add that for us any possible investigation of it is cut off by the lasting tongue-tie of—him—in yonder," again designating the mortuary stateroom. "The prisoner's deed—with that alone we have to do."

To this, and particularly the closing reiteration, the marine soldier, knowing not how aptly to reply, sadly abstained from saying aught. The first lieutenant, who at the outset had not unnaturally assumed primacy in the court, now overrulingly instructed by a glance from Captain Vere, a glance more effective than words, resumed that primacy. Turning to the prisoner, "Budd," he said, and scarce in equable tones, "Budd, if you have aught further to say for yourself, say it now."

Upon this the young sailor turned another quick glance toward Captain Vere; then, as taking a hint from that aspect, a hint confirming his own instinct that silence was now best, replied to the lieutenant, "I have said all, sir."

The marine—the same who had been the sentinel without the cabin door at the time that the foretopman, followed by the master-at-arms, entered it—he, standing by the sailor throughout these judicial proceedings, was now directed to take him back to the after compartment originally assigned to the prisoner and his custodian. As the twain disappeared from view, the three officers, as partially liberated from some inward constraint associated with Billy's mere presence, simultaneously stirred in their seats. They exchanged looks of troubled indecision, yet feeling that decide they must and without long delay. For Captain Vere, he for the time stood—unconsciously with his back toward them, apparently in one of his absent fits—gazing out from a sashed porthole to windward upon the monotonous blank of the twilight sea. But the court's silence continuing, broken only at moments by brief consultations, in low earnest tones, this served to arouse him and energize him. Turning, he to-and-fro paced the cabin athwart; in the returning ascent to windward climbing the slant deck in the ship's lee roll, without knowing it symbolizing thus in his action a mind resolute to surmount difficulties even if against primitive instincts strong as the wind and the sea. Presently he came to a stand before the three. After scanning their faces he stood less as mustering his thoughts for expression than as one inly deliberating how best to put them to well-meaning men not intellectually mature, men with whom it was necessary to demonstrate certain principles that were axioms to himself. Similar impatience as to talking is perhaps one reason that deters some minds from addressing any popular assemblies.

When speak he did, something, both in the substance of what he said and his manner of saying it, showed the influence of unshared studies modifying and tempering the practical training of an active career. This, along with his phraseology, now and then was suggestive of the grounds whereon rested that imputation of a certain pedantry socially alleged against him by certain naval men of wholly practical cast, captains who nevertheless would frankly concede that His Majesty's navy mustered no more efficient officer of their grade than Starry Vere.

What he said was to this effect: "Hitherto I have been but the witness, little more; and I should hardly think now to take another tone, that of your coadjutor for the time, did I not perceive in you—at the crisis too—a troubled hesitancy, proceeding, I doubt not, from the clash of military duty with moral scruple—scruple vitalized by compassion. For the compassion, how can I otherwise than share it? But, mindful of paramount obligations, I strive against scruples that may tend to enervate decision. Not, gentlemen, that I hide from myself that the case is an exceptional one. Speculatively regarded, it well might be referred to a jury of casuists.[7] But for us here, acting not as casuists or moralists, it is a case practical, and under martial law practically to be dealt with.

"But your scruples: do they move as in a dusk? Challenge them. Make them advance and declare themselves. Come now; do they import something like this: If, mindless of palliating circumstances, we are bound to regard the death of the master-at-arms as the prisoner's deed, then does that deed constitute a capital crime whereof the penalty is a mortal one. But in natural justice is nothing but the prisoner's overt act to be considered? How can we adjudge to summary and shameful death a fellow creature innocent before God, and whom we feel to be so?—Does that state it aright? You sign sad assent. Well, I too feel that, the full force of that. It is Nature. But do these buttons that we wear attest that our allegiance is to Nature? No, to the King. Though the ocean, which is inviolate Nature primeval, though this be the element where we move and have our being as sailors, yet as the King's officers lies our duty in a sphere correspondingly natural? So little is that true, that in receiving our commissions we in the most important regards ceased to be natural free agents. When war is declared are we the commissioned fighters previously consulted? We fight at command. If our judgments approve the war, that is but coincidence. So in other particulars. So now. For suppose condemnation to follow these present proceedings. Would it be so much we ourselves that would condemn as it would be martial law operating through us? For that law and the rigor of it, we are not responsible. Our vowed responsibility is in this: That however pitilessly that law may operate in any instances, we nevertheless adhere to it and administer it.

"But the exceptional in the matter moves the hearts within you. Even so too is mine moved. But let not warm hearts betray heads that should be cool. Ashore in a criminal case, will an upright judge allow himself off the bench to be waylaid by some tender kinswoman of the accused seeking to touch him with her tearful plea? Well, the heart here, sometimes the feminine in man, is as that piteous woman, and hard though it be, she must here be ruled out."

He paused, earnestly studying them for a moment; then resumed.

"But something in your aspect seems to urge that it is not solely the heart that moves in you, but also the conscience, the private conscience. But tell me whether or not, occupying the position we do, private conscience should not yield to that imperial one formulated in the code under which alone we officially proceed?"

Here the three men moved in their seats, less convinced than agitated by the course of an argument troubling but the more the spontaneous conflict within.

Perceiving which, the speaker paused for a moment; then abruptly changing his tone, went on.

"To steady us a bit, let us recur to the facts.—In wartime at sea a man-of-war's man strikes his superior in grade, and the blow kills. Apart from its effect the blow itself is, according to the Articles of War,[8] a capital crime. Furthermore—"

"Ay, sir," emotionally broke in the officer of marines, "in one sense it was. But surely Budd purposed neither mutiny nor homicide."

"Surely not, my good man. And before a court less arbitrary and more merciful than a martial one, that plea would largely extenuate. At the Last Assizes[9] it shall acquit. But how here? We proceed under the law of the Mutiny Act.[10] In feature no child can resemble his father more than that Act resembles in spirit the thing from which it derives—War. In His Majesty's service—in this ship, indeed—there are Englishmen forced to fight for the King against their will. Against their conscience, for aught we know. Though as their fellow creatures some of us may appreciate their position, yet as navy officers what reck we of it? Still less recks the enemy. Our impressed men he would fain cut down in the same swath with our volunteers. As regards the enemy's naval conscripts, some of whom may even share our own abhorrence of the regicidal French Directory, it is the same on our side. War looks but to the frontage, the appearance. And the Mutiny Act, War's child, takes after the father. Budd's intent or nonintent is nothing to the purpose.

"But while, put to it by those anxieties in you which I cannot but respect, I only repeat myself—while thus strangely we prolong proceedings that should be summary—the enemy may be sighted and an engagement result. We must do; and one of two things must we do—condemn or let go."

"Can we not convict and yet mitigate the penalty?" asked the sailing master, here speaking, and falteringly, for the first.

"Gentlemen, were that clearly lawful for us under the circumstances, consider the consequences of such clemency. The people" (meaning the ship's company) "have native sense; most of them are familiar with our naval usage and tradition; and how would they take it? Even could you explain to them—which our official position forbids—they, long molded by arbitrary discipline, have not that kind of intelligent responsiveness that might qualify them to comprehend and discriminate. No, to the people the foretopman's deed, however it be worded in the announcement, will be plain homicide committed in a flagrant act of mutiny. What penalty for that should follow, they know. But it does not follow. *Why?* they will ruminate. You know what sailors are. Will they not revert to the recent outbreak at the Nore? Ay. They know the well-founded alarm—the panic it struck throughout England. Your clement sentence they would account pusillanimous. They would think that we flinch, that we are afraid of them—afraid of practicing a lawful rigor singularly demanded at this juncture, lest it should provoke new troubles. What shame to us such a conjecture on their part, and how deadly to discipline. You see then, whither, prompted by duty and the law, I steadfastly drive. But I beseech you, my friends, do not take me amiss. I feel as you do for this unfortunate boy. But did he know our hearts, I take him to be of that generous nature that he would feel even for us on whom in this military necessity so heavy a compulsion is laid."

With that, crossing the deck he resumed his place by the sashed porthole, tacitly leaving the three to come to a decision. On the cabin's opposite side the troubled court sat silent. Loyal lieges, plain and practical, though at bottom they dissented from some points Captain Vere had put to them, they were without the faculty, hardly had the inclination, to gainsay one whom they felt to be an earnest man, one too not less their superior in mind than in naval rank. But it is not improbable that even such of his words as were not without influence over them, less came home to them than his closing appeal to their instinct as sea officers: in the forethought he threw out as to the practical consequences to discipline, considering the unconfirmed tone of the fleet at the time, should a man-of-war's man's violent killing at sea of a superior in grade be allowed to pass for aught else than a capital crime demanding prompt infliction of the penalty.

Not unlikely they were brought to something more or less akin to that harassed frame of mind which in the year 1842 actuated the commander of the U.S. brig-of-war *Somers*[11] to resolve, under the so-called Articles of War, Articles modeled upon the English Mutiny Act, to resolve upon the execution at sea of a midshipman and two sailors as mutineers designing the seizure of the brig. Which resolution was carried out though in a time of peace and within not many days' sail of home. An act vindicated by a naval court of inquiry subsequently convened ashore. History, and here cited without comment. True, the circumstances on board the *Somers* were different from those on board the *Bellipotent*. But the urgency felt, well-warranted or otherwise, was much the same.

Says a writer whom few know,[12] "Forty years after a battle it is easy for a noncombatant to reason about how it ought to have been fought. It is another thing personally and under fire to have to direct the fighting while involved in the obscuring smoke of it. Much so with respect to other emergencies involving considerations both practical and moral, and when it is imperative promptly to act. The greater the fog the more it imperils the steamer, and speed is put on though at the hazard of running somebody down. Little ween the snug card players in the cabin of the responsibilities of the sleepless man on the bridge."

In brief, Billy Budd was formally convicted and sentenced to be hung at the yardarm in the early morning watch, it being now night. Otherwise, as is customary in such cases, the sentence would forthwith have been carried out. In wartime on the field or in the fleet, a mortal punishment decreed by a drumhead court—on the field sometimes decreed by but a nod from the general—follows without delay on the heel of conviction, without appeal.

It was Captain Vere himself who of his own motion communicated the finding of the court to the prisoner, for that purpose going to the compartment where he was in custody and bidding the marine there to withdraw for the time.

Beyond the communication of the sentence, what took place at this interview was never known. But in view of the character of the twain briefly closeted in that stateroom, each radically sharing in the rarer qualities of our nature—so rare indeed as to be all but incredible to average minds however much cultivated—some conjectures may be ventured.

It would have been in consonance with the spirit of Captain Vere should he on this occasion have concealed nothing from the condemned one—should he indeed have frankly disclosed to him the part he himself had played in bringing about the decision, at the same time revealing his actuating motives. On Billy's side it is not improbable that such a confession would have been received in much the same spirit that prompted it. Not without a sort of joy, indeed, he might have appreciated the brave opinion of him implied in his captain's making such a confidant of him. Nor, as to the sentence itself, could he have been insensible that it was imparted to him as to one not afraid to die. Even more may have been. Captain Vere in end may have developed the passion sometimes latent under an exterior stoical or indifferent. He was old enough to have been Billy's father. The austere devotee of military duty, letting himself melt back into what remains primeval in our formalized humanity, may in end have caught Billy to his heart, even as Abraham may have caught young Isaac on the brink of resolutely offering him up in obedience to the exacting behest.[1] But there is no telling the sacrament, seldom if in any case revealed to the gadding world, wherever under circumstances at all akin to those here attempted to be set forth two of great Nature's nobler order embrace. There is privacy at the

time, inviolable to the survivor; and holy oblivion, the
sequel to each diviner magnanimity, providentially covers
all at last.

The first to encounter Captain Vere in act of leaving the
compartment was the senior lieutenant. The face he
beheld, for the moment one expressive of the agony of the
strong, was to that officer, though a man of fifty, a startling
revelation. That the condemned one suffered less than he
who mainly had effected the condemnation was apparently indicated by the former's exclamation in the scene
soon perforce to be touched upon.

23

Of a series of incidents within a brief term rapidly
following each other, the adequate narration may take up
a term less brief, especially if explanation or comment
here and there seem requisite to the better understanding
of such incidents. Between the entrance into the cabin of
him who never left it alive, and him who when he did leave
it left it as one condemned to die; between this and the
closeted interview just given, less than an hour and a half
had elapsed. It was an interval long enough, however, to
awaken speculations among no few of the ship's company
as to what it was that could be detaining in the cabin the
master-at-arms and the sailor; for a rumor that both of
them had been seen to enter it and neither of them had
been seen to emerge, this rumor had got abroad upon the
gun decks and in the tops, the people of a great warship
being in one respect like villagers, taking microscopic note
of every outward movement or nonmovement going on.
When therefore, in weather not at all tempestuous, all
hands were called in the second dogwatch, a summons
under such circumstances not usual in those hours, the
crew were not wholly unprepared for some announcement
extraordinary, one having connection too with the continued absence of the two men from their wonted haunts.

There was a moderate sea at the time; and the moon,

newly risen and near to being at its full, silvered the white
spar deck wherever not blotted by the clear-cut shadows
horizontally thrown of fixtures and moving men. On
either side the quarter-deck the marine guard under arms
was drawn up; and Captain Vere, standing in his place
surrounded by all the wardroom officers,[1] addressed his
men. In so doing, his manner showed neither more nor
less than that properly pertaining to his supreme position
aboard his own ship. In clear terms and concise he told
them what had taken place in the cabin: that the master-
at-arms was dead, that he who had killed him had been
already tried by a summary court and condemned to
death, and that the execution would take place in the early
morning watch. The word *mutiny* was not named in what
he said. He refrained too from making the occasion an
opportunity for any preachment as to the maintenance of
discipline, thinking perhaps that under existing circumstances in the navy the consequence of violating discipline
should be made to speak for itself.

Their captain's announcement was listened to by the
throng of standing sailors in a dumbness like that of a
seated congregation of believers in hell listening to the
clergyman's announcement of his Calvinistic text.

At the close, however, a confused murmur went up. It
began to wax. All but instantly, then, at a sign, it was
pierced and suppressed by shrill whistles of the boatswain
and his mates. The word was given to about ship.

To be prepared for burial Claggart's body was delivered
to certain petty officers of his mess. And here, not to clog
the sequel with lateral matters, it may be added that at a
suitable hour, the master-at-arms was committed to the
sea with every funeral honor properly belonging to his
naval grade.

In this proceeding as in every public one growing out of
the tragedy strict adherence to usage was observed. Nor in
any point could it have been at all deviated from, either
with respect to Claggart or Billy Budd, without begetting
undesirable speculations in the ship's company, sailors,
and more particularly men-of-war's men, being of all men
the greatest sticklers for usage. For similar cause, all

communication between Captain Vere and the condemned one ended with the closeted interview already given, the latter being now surrendered to the ordinary routine preliminary to the end. His transfer under guard from the captain's quarters was effected without unusual precautions—at least no visible ones. If possible, not to let the men so much as surmise that their officers anticipate aught amiss from them is the tacit rule in a military ship. And the more that some sort of trouble should really be apprehended, the more do the officers keep that apprehension to themselves, though not the less unostentatious vigilance may be augmented. In the present instance, the sentry placed over the prisoner had strict orders to let no one have communication with him but the chaplain. And certain unobtrusive measures were taken absolutely to insure this point.

24

In a seventy-four of the old order the deck known as the upper gun deck was the one covered over by the spar deck, which last, though not without its armament, was for the most part exposed to the weather. In general it was at all hours free from hammocks; those of the crew swinging on the lower gun deck and berth deck, the latter being not only a dormitory but also the place for the stowing of the sailors' bags, and on both sides lined with the large chests or movable pantries of the many messes of the men.

On the starboard side of the *Bellipotent*'s upper gun deck, behold Billy Budd under sentry lying prone in irons in one of the bays formed by the regular spacing of the guns comprising the batteries on either side. All these pieces were of the heavier caliber of that period. Mounted on lumbering wooden carriages, they were hampered with cumbersome harness of breeching and strong side-tackles for running them out. Guns and carriages, together with the long rammers and shorter linstocks[1] lodged in loops overhead—all these, as customary, were painted black;

and the heavy hempen breechings, tarred to the same tint, wore the like livery of the undertakers. In contrast with the funereal hue of these surroundings, the prone sailor's exterior apparal, white jumper and white duck trousers, each more or less soiled, dimly glimmered in the obscure light of the bay like a patch of discolored snow in early April lingering at some upland cave's black mouth. In effect he is already in his shroud, or the garments that shall serve him in lieu of one. Over him but scarce illuminating him, two battle lanterns swing from two massive beams of the deck above. Fed with the oil supplied by the war contractors (whose gains, honest or otherwise, are in every land an anticipated portion of the harvest of death), with flickering splashes of dirty yellow light they pollute the pale moonshine all but ineffectually struggling in obstructed flecks through the open ports from which the tampioned cannon protrude. Other lanterns at intervals serve but to bring out somewhat the obscurer bays which, like small confessionals or side-chapels in a cathedral, branch from the long dim-vistaed broad aisle between the two batteries of that covered tier.

Such was the deck where now lay the Handsome Sailor. Through the rose-tan of his complexion no pallor could have shown. It would have taken days of sequestration from the winds and the sun to have brought about the effacement of that. But the skeleton in the cheekbone at the point of its angle was just beginning delicately to be defined under the warm-tinted skin. In fervid hearts self-contained, some brief experiences devour our human tissue as secret fire in a ship's hold consumes cotton in the bale.

But now lying between the two guns, as nipped in the vice of fate, Billy's agony, mainly proceeding from a generous young heart's virgin experience of the diabolical incarnate and effective in some men—the tension of that agony was over now. It survived not the something healing in the closeted interview with Captain Vere. Without movement, he lay as in a trance, that adolescent expression previously noted as his taking on something akin to the look of a slumbering child in the cradle when the warm hearth-glow of the still chamber at night plays on the dimples that at whiles mysteriously form in the cheek, silently coming and going there. For now and then in the gyved[2] one's trance a serene happy light born of some wandering reminiscence or dream would diffuse itself over his face, and then wane away only anew to return.

The chaplain, coming to see him and finding him thus, and perceiving no sign that he was conscious of his presence, attentively regarded him for a space, then slipping aside, withdrew for the time, peradventure feeling that even he, the minister of Christ though receiving his stipend from Mars,[3] had no consolation to proffer which could result in a peace transcending that which he beheld. But in the small hours he came again. And the prisoner, now awake to his surroundings, noticed his approach, and civilly, all but cheerfully, welcomed him. But it was to little purpose that in the interview following, the good man sought to bring Billy Budd to some godly understanding that he must die, and at dawn. True, Billy himself freely referred to his death as a thing close at hand; but it was something in the way that children will refer to death in general, who yet among their other sports will play a funeral with hearse and mourners.

Not that like children Billy was incapable of conceiving what death really is. No, but he was wholly without irrational fear of it, a fear more prevalent in highly civilized communities than those so-called barbarous ones which in all respects stand nearer to unadulterate Nature. And, as elsewhere said, a barbarian Billy radically was— as much so, for all the costume, as his countrymen the British captives, living trophies, made to march in the Roman triumph of Germanicus.[4] Quite as much so as those later barbarians, young men probably, and picked specimens among the earlier British converts to Christianity, at least nominally such, taken to Rome (as today converts from lesser isles of the sea may be taken to London), of whom the Pope of that time,[5] admiring the strangeness of their personal beauty so unlike the Italian stamp, their clear ruddy complexion and curled flaxen locks, exclaimed, "Angles" (meaning *English*, the modern derivative), "Angles, do you call them? And is it because they look so like angels?" Had it been later in time, one would think that the Pope had in mind Fra Angelico's seraphs,[6] some of whom, plucking apples in gardens of the Hesperides,[7] have the faint rosebud complexion of the more beautiful English girls.

If in vain the good chaplain sought to impress the young barbarian with ideas of death akin to those conveyed in the skull, dial, and crossbones on old tombstones, equally futile to all appearance were his efforts to bring home to him the thought of salvation and a Savior. Billy listened, but less out of awe or reverence, perhaps, than from a certain natural politeness, doubtless at bottom regarding all that in much the same way that most mariners of his class take any discourse abstract or out of the common tone of the workaday world. And this sailor way of taking clerical discourse is not wholly unlike the way in which the primer of Christianity, full of transcendent miracles, was received long ago on tropic isles by any superior *savage,* so called—a Tahitian, say, of Captain Cook's time[8] or shortly after that time. Out of natural courtesy he received, but did not appropriate. It was like a gift placed in the palm of an outreached hand upon which the fingers do not close.

But the *Bellipotent's* chaplain was a discreet man possessing the good sense of a good heart. So he insisted not in his vocation here. At the instance of Captain Vere, a lieutenant had apprised him of pretty much everything as to Billy; and since he felt that innocence was even a better thing than religion wherewith to go to Judgment, he reluctantly withdrew; but in his emotion not without first performing an act strange enough in an Englishman, and under the circumstances yet more so in any regular priest. Stooping over, he kissed on the fair cheek his fellow man, a felon in martial law, one whom though on the confines of death he felt he could never convert to a dogma; nor for all that did he fear for his future.

Marvel not that having been made acquainted with the young sailor's essential innocence the worthy man lifted not a finger to avert the doom of such a martyr to martial discipline. So to do would not only have been as idle as invoking the desert, but would also have been an audacious transgression of the bounds of his function, one as exactly prescribed to him by military law as that of the boatswain or any other naval officer. Bluntly put, a chaplain is the minister of the Prince of Peace serving in the host of the God of War—Mars. As such, he is as incongruous as a musket would be on the altar at Christmas. Why, then, is he there? Because he indirectly subserves the purpose attested by the cannon; because too he lends the sanction of the religion of the meek to that which practically is the abrogation of everything but brute Force.

25

The night so luminous on the spar deck, but otherwise on the cavernous ones below, levels so like the tiered galleries in a coal mine—the luminous night passed away. But like the prophet in the chariot disappearing in heaven and dropping his mantle to Elisha,[1] the withdrawing night transferred its pale robe to the breaking day. A meek, shy light appeared in the East, where stretched a diaphanous fleece of white furrowed vapor. That light slowly waxed. Suddenly *eight bells* was struck aft, responded to by one louder metallic stroke from forward. It was four o'clock in the morning. Instantly the silver whistles were heard summoning all hands to witness punishment. Up through the great hatchways rimmed with racks of heavy shot the watch below came pouring, overspreading with the watch already on deck the space between the mainmast and foremast including that occupied by the capacious launch and the black booms tiered on either side of it, boat and booms making a summit of observation for the powderboys and younger tars. A different group comprising one watch of topmen leaned over the rail of that sea balcony, no small one in a seventy-four, looking down on the crowd below. Man or boy, none spake but in whisper, and few spake at all. Captain Vere—as before, the central figure among the assembled commissioned officers—stood nigh the break of the poop deck facing forward. Just below him on the quarter-deck the marines in full equipment were drawn up much as at the scene of the promulgated sentence.

At sea in the old time, the execution by halter of a military sailor was generally from the foreyard. In the present instance, for special reasons the mainyard was assigned. Under an arm of that yard the prisoner was presently brought up, the chaplain attending him. It was noted at the time, and remarked upon afterwards, that in this final scene the good man evinced little or nothing of the perfunctory. Brief speech indeed he had with the condemned one, but the genuine Gospel was less on his tongue than in his aspect and manner towards him. The final preparations personal to the latter being speedily brought to an end by two boatswain's mates, the consummation impended. Billy stood facing aft. At the penultimate moment, his words, his only ones, words wholly unobstructed in the utterance, were these: "God bless Captain Vere!" Syllables so unanticipated coming from one with the ignominious hemp about his neck—a conventional felon's benediction directed aft towards the quarters of honor; syllables too delivered in the clear melody of a singing bird on the point of launching from the twig—had a phenomenal effect, not unenhanced by the rare personal beauty of the young sailor, spiritualized now through late experiences so poignantly profound.

Without volition, as it were, as if indeed the ship's populace were but the vehicles of some vocal current electric, with one voice from alow and aloft came a resonant sympathetic echo: "God bless Captain Vere!" And yet at that instant Billy alone must have been in their hearts, even as in their eyes.

At the pronounced words and the spontaneous echo that voluminously rebounded them, Captain Vere, either through stoic self-control or a sort of momentary paralysis induced by emotional shock, stood erectly rigid as a musket in the ship-armorer's rack.

The hull, deliberately recovering from the periodic roll to leeward, was just regaining an even keel when the last signal, a preconcerted dumb one, was given. At the same moment it chanced that the vapory fleece hanging low in

the East was shot through with a soft glory as of the fleece
of the Lamb of God seen in mystical vision,[2] and simultaneously therewith, watched by the wedged mass of up-
turned faces, Billy ascended; and, ascending, took the full
rose of the dawn.[3]

In the pinioned figure arrived at the yard-end, to the
wonder of all no motion was apparent, none save that
created by the slow roll of the hull in moderate weather, so
majestic in a great ship ponderously cannoned.

26

When some days afterwards, in reference to the singularity
just mentioned, the purser,[1] a rather ruddy, rotund person
more accurate as an accountant than profound as a
philosopher, said at mess to the surgeon, "What testimony
to the force lodged in will power," the latter, saturnine,
spare, and tall, one in whom a discreet causticity went
along with a manner less genial than polite, replied, "Your
pardon, Mr. Purser. In a hanging scientifically con-
ducted—and under special orders I myself directed how
Budd's was to be effected—any movement following the
completed suspension and originating in the body suspended, such movement indicates mechanical spasm in
the muscular system. Hence the absence of that is no more
attributable to will power, as you call it, than to horse-
power—begging your pardon."

"But this muscular spasm you speak of, is not that in a
degree more or less invariable in these cases?"

"Assuredly so, Mr. Purser."

"How then, my good sir, do you account for its absence
in this instance?"

"Mr. Purser, it is clear that your sense of the singularity
in this matter equals not mine. You account for it by what
you call will power—a term not yet included in the
lexicon of science. For me, I do not, with my present
knowledge, pretend to account for it at all. Even should we
assume the hypothesis that at the first touch of the
halyards the action of Budd's heart, intensified by extraor-

dinary emotion at its climax, abruptly stopped—much like a watch when in carelessly winding it up you strain at the finish, thus snapping the chain—even under that hypothesis how account for the phenomenon that followed?"

"You admit, then, that the absence of spasmodic movement was phenomenal."

"It was phenomenal, Mr. Purser, in the sense that it was an appearance the cause of which is not immediately to be assigned."

"But tell me, my dear sir," pertinaciously continued the other, "was the man's death effected by the halter, or was it a species of euthanasia?"[2]

"*Euthanasia,* Mr. Purser, is something like your *will power:* I doubt its authenticity as a scientific term—begging your pardon again. It is at once imaginative and metaphysical—in short, Greek—But," abruptly changing his tone, "there is a case in the sick bay that I do not care to leave to my assistants. Beg your pardon, but excuse me." And rising from the mess he formally withdrew.

27

The silence at the moment of execution and for a moment or two continuing thereafter, a silence but emphasized by the regular wash of the sea against the hull or the flutter of a sail caused by the helmsman's eyes being tempted astray, this emphasized silence was gradually disturbed by a sound not easily to be verbally rendered. Whoever has heard the freshet-wave of a torrent suddenly swelled by pouring showers in tropical mountains, showers not shared by the plain; whoever has heard the first muffled murmur of its sloping advance through precipitous woods may form some conception of the sound now heard. The seeming remoteness of its source was because of its murmurous indistinctness, since it came from close by, even from the men massed on the ship's open deck. Being inarticulate, it was dubious in significance further than it seemed to indicate some capricious revulsion of thought or feeling such as mobs ashore are liable to, in the present instance possibly implying a sullen revocation on the men's part of their involuntary echoing of Billy's benediction. But ere the murmur had time to wax into clamor it was met by a strategic command, the more telling that it came with abrupt unexpectedness: "Pipe down the starboard watch, Boatswain, and see that they go."

Shrill as the shriek of the sea hawk, the silver whistles of the boatswain and his mates pierced that ominous low sound, dissipating it; and yielding to the mechanism of discipline the throng was thinned by one-half. For the remainder, most of them were set to temporary employments connected with trimming the yards and so forth, business readily to be got up to serve occasion by any officer of the deck.

Now each proceeding that follows a mortal sentence pronounced at sea by a drumhead court is characterized by promptitude not perceptibly merging into hurry, though bordering that. The hammock, the one which had been Billy's bed when alive, having already been ballasted with shot and otherwise prepared to serve for his canvas coffin, the last offices of the sea undertakers, the sailmaker's mates, were now speedily completed. When everything was in readiness a second call for all hands, made necessary by the strategic movement before mentioned, was sounded, now to witness burial.

The details of this closing formality it needs not to give. But when the tilted plank let slide its freight into the sea, a second strange human murmur was heard, blended now with another inarticulate sound proceeding from certain larger seafowl who, their attention having been attracted by the peculiar commotion in the water resulting from the heavy sloped dive of the shotted hammock into the sea, flew screaming to the spot. So near the hull did they come, that the stridor or bony creak of their gaunt double-jointed pinions was audible. As the ship under light airs passed on, leaving the burial spot astern, they still kept circling it low down with the moving shadow of their outstretched wings and the croaked requiem of their cries.

Upon sailors as superstitious as those of the age preceding ours, men-of-war's men too who had just beheld the prodigy of repose in the form suspended in air, and now foundering in the deeps; to such mariners the action of the seafowl, though dictated by mere animal greed for prey, was big with no prosaic significance. An uncertain movement began among them, in which some encroachment was made. It was tolerated but for a moment. For suddenly the drum beat to quarters, which familiar sound happening at least twice every day, had upon the present occasion a signal peremptoriness in it. True martial discipline long continued superinduces in average man a sort of impulse whose operation at the official word of command much resembles in its promptitude the effect of an instinct.

The drumbeat dissolved the multitude, distributing most of them along the batteries of the two covered gun decks. There, as wonted, the guns' crews stood by their respective cannon erect and silent. In due course the first officer, sword under arm and standing in his place on the quarter-deck, formally received the successive reports of the sworded lieutenants commanding the sections of batteries below; the last of which reports being made, the summed report he delivered with the customary salute to the commander. All this occupied time, which in the present case was the object in beating to quarters at an hour prior to the customary one. That such variance from usage was authorized by an officer like Captain Vere, a martinet as some deemed him, was evidence of the necessity for unusual action implied in what he deemed to be temporarily the mood of his men. "With mankind," he would say, "forms, measured forms, are everything; and that is the import couched in the story of Orpheus[1] with his lyre spellbinding the wild denizens of the wood." And this he once applied to the disruption of forms going on across the Channel and the consequences thereof.

At this unwonted muster at quarters, all proceeded as at the regular hour. The band on the quarter-deck played a sacred air, after which the chaplain went through the customary morning service. That done, the drum beat the retreat; and toned by music and religious rites subserving the discipline and purposes of war, the men in their wonted orderly manner dispersed to the places alloted them when not at the guns.

And now it was full day. The fleece of low-hanging vapor had vanished, licked up by the sun that late had so glorified it. And the circumambient air in the clearness of its serenity was like smooth white marble in the polished block not yet removed from the marble-dealer's yard.

28

The symmetry of form attainable in pure fiction cannot so readily be achieved in a narration essentially having less to do with fable than with fact. Truth uncompromisingly told will always have its ragged edges; hence the conclusion of such a narration is apt to be less finished than an architectural finial.[1]

How it fared with the Handsome Sailor during the year of the Great Mutiny has been faithfully given. But though properly the story ends with his life, something in way of sequel will not be amiss. Three brief chapters will suffice.

In the general rechristening under the Directory of the craft originally forming the navy of the French monarchy, the *St. Louis* line-of-battle ship was named the *Athée* (the *Atheist*). Such a name, like some other substituted ones in the Revolutionary fleet, while proclaiming the infidel audacity of the ruling power, was yet, though not so intended to be, the aptest name, if one consider it, ever given to a warship; far more so indeed than the *Devastation,* the *Erebus* (the *Hell*), and similar names bestowed upon fighting ships.

On the return passage to the English fleet from the detached cruise during which occurred the events already recorded, the *Bellipotent* fell in with the *Athée*. An engagement ensued, during which Captain Vere, in the act of putting his ship alongside the enemy with a view of throwing his boarders across her bulwarks, was hit by a musket ball from a porthole of the enemy's main cabin.

More than disabled, he dropped to the deck and was carried below to the same cockpit where some of his men already lay. The senior lieutenant took command. Under him the enemy was finally captured, and though much crippled was by rare good fortune successfully taken into Gibraltar, an English port not very distant from the scene of the fight. There, Captain Vere with the rest of the wounded was put ashore. He lingered for some days, but the end came. Unhappily he was cut off too early for the Nile and Trafalgar. The spirit that 'spite its philosophic austerity may yet have indulged in the most secret of all passions, ambition, never attained to the fullness of fame.

Not long before death, while lying under the influence of that magical drug[2] which, soothing the physical frame, mysteriously operates on the subtler element in man, he was heard to murmur words inexplicable to his attendant: "Billy Budd, Billy Budd." That these were not the accents of remorse would seem clear from what the attendant said to the *Bellipotent*'s senior officer of marines, who, as the most reluctant to condemn of the members of the drumhead court, too well knew, though here he kept the knowledge to himself, who Billy Budd was.

29

Some few weeks after the execution, among other matters under the head of "News from the Mediterranean," there appeared in a naval chronicle of the time, an authorized weekly publication, an account of the affair.[1] It was doubtless for the most part written in good faith, though the medium, partly rumor, through which the facts must have reached the writer served to deflect and in part falsify them. The account was as follows:

"On the tenth of the last month a deplorable occurrence took place on board H.M.S. *Bellipotent*. John Claggart, the ship's master-at-arms, discovering that some sort of plot was incipient among an inferior section of the ship's company, and that the ringleader was one William Budd;

he, Claggart, in the act of arraigning the man before the captain, was vindictively stabbed to the heart by the suddenly drawn sheath knife of Budd.

"The deed and the implement employed sufficiently suggest that though mustered into the service under an English name the assassin was no Englishman, but one of those aliens adopting English cognomens whom the present extraordinary necessities of the service have caused to be admitted into it in considerable numbers.

"The enormity of the crime and the extreme depravity of the criminal appear the greater in view of the character of the victim, a middle-aged man respectable and discreet, belonging to that minor official grade, the petty officers, upon whom, as none know better than the commissioned gentlemen, the efficiency of His Majesty's navy so largely depends. His function was a responsible one, at once onerous and thankless; and his fidelity in it the greater because of his strong patriotic impulse. In this instance as in so many other instances in these days, the character of this unfortunate man signally refutes, if refutation were needed, that peevish saying attributed to the late Dr. Johnson, that patriotism is the last refuge of a scoundrel.

"The criminal paid the penalty of his crime. The promptitude of the punishment has proved salutary. Nothing amiss is now apprehended aboard H.M.S. *Bellipotent*."

The above, appearing in a publication now long ago superannuated and forgotten, is all that hitherto has stood in human record to attest what manner of men respectively were John Claggart and Billy Budd.

30

Everything is for a term venerated in navies. Any tangible object associated with some striking incident of the service is converted into a monument. The spar from which the foretopman was suspended was for some few years kept trace of by the bluejackets. Their knowledges followed it from ship to dockyard and again from dockyard to ship, still pursuing it even when at last reduced to a mere dockyard boom. To them a chip of it was as a piece of the Cross. Ignorant though they were of the secret facts of the tragedy, and not thinking but that the penalty was somehow unavoidably inflicted from the naval point of view, for all that, they instinctively felt that Billy was a sort of man as incapable of mutiny as of wilful murder. They recalled the fresh young image of the Handsome Sailor, that face never deformed by a sneer or subtler vile freak of the heart within. This impression of him was doubtless deepened by the fact that he was gone, and in a measure mysteriously gone. On the gun decks of the *Bellipotent* the general estimate of his nature and its unconscious simplicity eventually found rude utterance from another foretopman, one of his own watch, gifted, as some sailors are, with an artless *poetic* temperament. The tarry hand made some lines which, after circulating among the shipboard crews for a while, finally got rudely printed at Portsmouth as a ballad. The title given to it was the sailor's.

BILLY IN THE DARBIES[1]

Good of the chaplain to enter Lone Bay
And down on his marrowbones here and pray
For the likes just o' me, Billy Budd.—But, look:
Through the port comes the moonshine astray!
It tips the guard's cutlass and silvers this nook;
But 'twill die in the dawning of Billy's last day.
A jewel-block they'll make of me tomorrow,
Pendant pearl from the yardarm-end
Like the eardrop I gave to Bristol Molly—
O, 'tis me, not the sentence they'll suspend.
Ay, ay, all is up; and I must up too,
Early in the morning, aloft from alow.
On an empty stomach now never it would do.
They'll give me a nibble—bit o' biscuit ere I go.
Sure, a messmate will reach me the last parting cup;
But, turning heads away from the hoist and the
 belay,
Heaven knows who will have the running of me up!

No pipe to those halyards.—But aren't it all sham?
A blur's in my eyes; it is dreaming that I am.
A hatchet to my hawser? All adrift to go?
The drum roll to grog, and Billy never know?
But Donald he has promised to stand by the plank;
So I'll shake a friendly hand ere I sink.
But—no! It is dead then I'll be, come to think.
I remember Taff the Welshman when he sank.
And his cheek it was like the budding pink.
But me they'll lash in hammock, drop me deep.
Fathoms down, fathoms down, how I'll dream fast
     asleep.
I feel it stealing now. Sentry, are you there?
Just ease these darbies at the wrist,
And roll me over fair!
I am sleepy, and the oozy weeds about me twist.

Literary Allusions and Notes

Half title

1. *Billy Budd, Sailor (An Inside Narrative)*: When first published in 1924, Melville's novel was edited by Raymond Weaver, who gave it the title *Billy Budd, Foretopman: What befell him in the year of the Great Mutiny &c.* In the revised 1962 text edited by Harrison Hayford and Merton Sealts, Jr. and used here, the title that appears on the first page of the manuscript is restored. By "inside narrative" Melville seems to mean an account that can reveal the inward truth of the case, as opposed to the accounts that appear in official reports, newspapers, or romanticized poems. Specifically, the "inside narrative" that we are reading should be contrasted to the account that appears in section 29, reported from "a naval chronicle of the time." In addition to the change of title, the Hayford-Sealts text differs from earlier texts in wording and punctuation. It also omits two paragraphs on the background of the age mistakenly thought to be Melville's preface to the story, as well as two superseded leaves discussing Claggart's depravity, which Weaver had included in his chapter 11 and Freeman had assigned to a chapter 12. A final change is discussed in note 10 to chapter 1.

Dedication

1. "Jack Chase": A shipmate of Melville's on the frigate *United States* and a major character in the novel *White-Jacket* (1850). F. Barron Freeman, one of the early editors of *Billy Budd*, suggested that Chase was a model for the

"Handsome Sailor." In *White-Jacket*, Melville describes Chase as "a stickler for the Rights of Man, and the liberties of the world." The ship from which Billy is taken is called the *Rights-of-Man*; see note 13 to chapter 1.

Chapter I

1. "Aldebaran": Brightest star in the constellation Taurus, where it forms the bull's eye.

2. "blood of Ham": Ham was the son of Noah and the father of Canaan; in Genesis 9:25, Noah cursed Canaan and his descendants after Canaan saw his grandfather naked and drunk in his tent. This curse was often cited by white Westerners as a justification for slavery; Melville here is stressing the contrast between this stereotype and the natural nobility of this African sailor.

3. "Anacharsis Cloots": Jean-Baptiste du Val de Grâce, Baron de Cloots (1755–1794) was a Prussian-born revolutionary, known to Melville through Thomas Carlyle's *The French Revolution*. Carlyle described Cloots as introducing a representative assortment of men before the French National Assembly as a show of support for the French Revolution. Carlyle described these men as "mute representatives of their tongue-tied, befettered, heavy-laden Nations." Melville describes the multiracial crew of the *Pequod* in *Moby-Dick* as an "Anacharsis Clootz deputation."

4. "pagod": Idol.

5. "Murat": A dandy; a reference to Joachim Murat (1767?–1815), who was made king of Naples by Napoleon.

6. "the tempestuous Erie Canal": A joke, since the Erie Canal is a calm commercial waterway in New York State.

7. "Alexander curbing the fiery Bucephalus": This story is told in Plutarch's *Lives*. Alexander the Great of Greece (356–323 B.C.) fulfilled the prophecy of an oracle by taming the wild horse Bucephalus, whose name means "bull-head."

8. "welkin": Sky; since the sky is blue, "welkin-eyed" means "blue-eyed."

9. "impressed on the Narrow Seas": Impressment was

the drafting of sailors from merchant ships or from ashore, and it was a common practice in the English Navy during the Napoleonic Wars. "Narrow Seas" refers to the English Channel and St. George's Channel.

10. "a seventy-four outward bound, H.M.S. *Bellipotent*": The name means "powerful in war." Melville had originally called the ship the *Indomitable,* suggesting courage, but in later drafts of *Billy Budd* changed the name to the less positively charged *Bellipotent,* which suggests brute force rather than bravery. "Seventy-four" refers to the number of guns on the warship.

11. "shipmaster": Captain.

12. "shindy": Brawl.

13. "the *Rights-of-Man*": Thomas Paine's tract *The Rights of Man* (1791) was written in response to Edmund Burke's conservative *Reflections on the Revolution in France* (1790). Burke's book argued for the priority of social institutions, Paine's for the priority of natural rights. Thus, in moving from the merchant ship to the man-of-war, Billy leaves behind his natural rights and enters into the authoritarian and repressive world of martial law.

14. "Voltaire, Diderot, and so forth": Voltaire (1694–1778) was the author of the famous philosophical novel *Candide* (1759) and a contributor to the *Encyclopédie, ou Dictionnaire raisonné des sciences, des arts et des métiers* (Encyclopedia, or Methodical Dictionary of the Sciences, Arts and Trades, 1751–1780) edited chiefly by Denis Diderot (1713–1784). Both were part of a group of eighteenth-century French thinkers referred to as the *philosophes,* whose belief in the supremacy of human reason was a cornerstone of Enlightenment thought. The *Encyclopédie* was an attempt to classify all human knowledge systematically and was marked by skepticism toward religion and by contempt for anything that seemed to partake of superstition.

15. "sinister dexterity": An example of what Melville calls "double meanings" in the next sentence. The phrase is an ironic play on etymological roots: the Latin *sinister* means "having to do with the left hand," while *dexter* means "having to do with the right hand."

16. "foretop": The platform at the head of the foremast.

17. "mess": Group of sailors assigned to eat together.

18. "the last dogwatch": 6:00 to 8:00 P.M.

Chapter 2

1. "by-blow": Bastard child.

2. "any trace of the wisdom of the serpent, nor yet quite a dove": In Matthew 10:16, Christ tells his disciples, "Behold, I send you forth as sheep in the midst of wolves: be ye therefore wise as serpents, and harmless as doves."

3. "doxies": Prostitutes.

4. "Cain's city and citified man": After killing his brother Abel, Cain was banished from the face of God and forced to leave the countryside. He founded a city in the land of Nod (Genesis 4: 13–17).

5. "Caspar Hauser": A foundling (1812?–1833), possibly amnesiac, who was discovered on the streets of Nuremberg in 1828 and claimed to have been kept prisoner in a hole. He was stabbed to death by a man thought to have promised him information about his origins, who may in fact have been his former captor. He was believed to have had noble origin and was often invoked as a symbol of the innocence of humankind in the state of nature.

6. "Honest and poor . . . brought?": From the *Epigrams* (1.4.1–2) of the Roman satiric poet Martial (first century A.D.), as translated by Cowley in the Bohn edition (1865).

7. "the beautiful woman in one of Hawthorne's minor tales": A reference to Georgiana in "The Birth-mark," whose only sign of human imperfection is a small hand-shaped birthmark on her left cheek. "Minor" here means "shorter."

8. "the envious marplot of Eden": Satan.

Chapter 3

1. "at Spithead . . . at the Nore": Two insurrections within the British fleet that were symptomatic of the

political turmoil of the times. In 1797, Britain's continental allies had either been defeated or had withdrawn from the war, and the French were masters of western Europe. The fleets of France, Spain, and Holland were allied against Great Britain. Though the Spanish line was broken at the battle of Cape St. Vincent in February 1797, the whole naval position in the North Sea was threatened by mutinies in the fleet. The first mutiny occurred at Spithead (a "roadstead" or protected anchorage in the English Channel between Portsmouth and the Isle of Wight) on April 15. It was fueled by the grievances of sailors who felt that they were badly fed, seldom paid, brutally punished to maintain discipline, and often forced into the navy through impressment. The authorities granted the sailors' claims, and Parliament voted to raise seamen's pay. This action, together with a royal pardon, brought an end to the mutiny, but it was followed by another on May 12 in the North Sea fleet, which was blockading the Dutch coast. Mutineers seized the ships and sailed back to the Nore, a sandbank at the mouth of the Thames. The men returned to their duties after a month, and the ringleader and eighteen others were hanged. The two mutinies form a crucial historical context for the action of *Billy Budd, Sailor*: they influence Captain Vere's decision to act quickly and to follow what he believes to be the letter of military law, in order to maintain strict military discipline and avert the chance of mutiny.

2. "French Directory": A body of five that functioned as France's chief executive from 1795 to 1799.

3. "the famous signal": Melville is referring to Admiral Horatio Nelson's signal to the fleet at the Battle of Trafalgar in 1805: "England expects that every man will do his duty." Lord Nelson himself was mortally wounded in the victory.

4. "roadstead": Protected anchorage.

5. "France in Flames": A reference to the Reign of Terror (1793–1794) and its aftermath.

6. "Dibdin": Charles Dibdin (1745–1814), English playwright and songwriter whose chauvinistic celebrations of sailor life Melville admired for what he called their "sea chivalry and romance."

7. "William James": British historian (d. 1827), author of *Naval History of Great Britain* (1860).

8. "Red Flag": A sign of revolution.

9. "a coronet for Nelson . . . Trafalgar": According to Robert Southey's *Life of Nelson*, which Melville owned and used as a source, Nelson received a baron's coronet for his victory in the Battle of the Nile (1798). He led the British fleet to victory at the decisive Battle of Trafalgar (1805), destroying twenty French and Spanish ships while losing none of his own, but was mortally wounded (his heroic death invoked here as a "naval crown of crowns"). Melville uses Nelson as a foil for Vere: Nelson is both a great military hero and a great, magnanimous spirit, in contrast to Vere, who is able but spiritually and imaginatively constricted.

Chapter 4

1. "Don John . . . American Decaturs of 1812": Don John of Austria (1547–1578) was a commander for the Holy League at the Battle of Lepanto in 1571. Andrea Doria (1468–1560) led the Genoese fleet against the Turks. Maarten Tromp (1597–1653) commanded the Dutch fleet against the Spanish. Jean Bart (1650–1702) led French privateers against both the British and the Dutch. Stephen Decatur (1779–1820) fought against the British in the War of 1812.

2. "*Monitors*": In a famous Civil War sea battle, two ironclad boats—the Union *Monitor* and the Confederate *Merrimack*—engaged one another with inconclusive results off the coast of Virginia.

3. "Benthamites of war": Followers of the English Utilitarian philosopher Jeremy Bentham (1748–1832), who believed that "the greatest happiness of the greatest number is the foundation of morals and legislation." His attempt to create scientific scale to measure the relative importance of pleasure and pain in the making of moral decisions struck Melville as ignominious. Melville's poem "A Utilitarian View of the *Monitor*'s Fight," included in *Battle-Pieces and Aspects of the War* (1866), contrasts modern warfare with its impersonal technology to the

"pomp" and "glory" of what he calls the "lace and feather" days.

4. "at Copenhagen": The Danes believed they that they had thwarted Nelson in 1801 by removing the navigational buoys near Copenhagen, but Nelson simply replaced the buoys after taking new soundings.

5. "Wellington": Arthur Wellesley, first duke of Wellington (1769–1852), British general who defeated Napoleon at Waterloo. He served as prime minister from 1828 to 1830; his repressive policies were unpopular and caused riots.

6. "Alfred in his funeral ode": Alfred, Lord Tennyson (1809–1892), "Ode on the Death of the Duke of Wellington" (1852).

Chapter 5

1. "Mansfield": William Murray, Earl of Mansfield (1705–1793), became lord chief justice of Britain in 1756.

2. "Two Mutinies": Spithead and Nore.

3. "to shift his pennant": To relocate himself and his flag of office.

Chapter 6

1. "Vere": Vere's name is often read as a play on the Latin words *vir* (man) and *verus* (true), as well as on the word *severe.*

2. "De Grasse": British Admiral George Brydges, Baron Rodney (1719–1792), defeated the French admiral François de Grasse at a battle off Dominica in 1782; he was assisted by Sir William George Fairfax.

3. "the blank sea": At a crucial point in the trial scene (chapter 21), Vere will gaze out "upon the monotonous blank of the twilight sea," a reminder perhaps of the indifference of nature against which human institutions are a necessary but flawed bulwark.

4. "Andrew Marvell": English poet (1621–1678).

5. "starry Vere": Anne Fairfax Vere, whose daughter Mary had been tutored by Marvell.

Chapter 7

1. "Montaigne": Michel de Montaigne (1533–1592), French politician and essayist. Montaigne argued that human conduct should be governed by fixed, rational principles and insisted that people must live according to civil laws rather than according to conscience or free will. Melville suggests that Vere's reading has differentiated him from other men of his class and profession.

2. "journals": Newspapers.

Chapter 8

1. "petty officers": Roughly equivalent to noncommissioned officers in the army, these are lesser officers appointed by the ship's captain.

2. "Tecumseh": Shawnee Indian chief (1768?–1813) who tried to unite Indian tribes in Florida and sided with the British in the War of 1812. He was defeated at Tippecanoe by William Henry Harrison.

3. "Titus Oates:" A clergyman (1649–1705) who invented the story of a Catholic plot to assassinate Charles II, burn London, and massacre English Protestants in 1678. As a result of this so-called Popish Plot, many Catholics were persecuted and killed before Oates's story was exposed as a fabrication.

4. "phrenologically associated": Phrenology was a fashionable pseudoscience that claimed to be able to determine character traits by studying the contours of the skull.

5. "incog": With concealed identity; incognito.

6. "chevalier": As used here, a swindler or confidence man.

7. "King's Bench": A court of law.

8. "press gangs": Gangs charged with rounding up men for ships, occasionally kidnapping them when necessary. See note 9 to chapter 1.

9. "a Trafalgar man": A veteran of the Battle of Trafalgar.

10. "harpies": In Greek mythology, fierce predatory birds with women's faces, who were daughters of the

Titaness Electra. They served as ministers of divine vengeance.

11. "fallen Bastille": Fourteenth-century Parisian fortress in use as a prison when it was stormed by French citizens on July 14, 1789, at the start of the French Revolution. July 14 is now marked as the holiday Bastille Day in France.

12. "Camoëns' Spirit of the Cape": In the *Lusiads* (1572), an epic written by the Portuguese poet Luiz de Camoëns (1525–1580), the monster Adamastor menaces Vasco da Gama and his crew as they round the Cape of Good Hope on their way to India.

13. "Bunker Hill": First great battle of the American Revolution, in Boston, Massachusetts, on June 17, 1775. Seeking to control the high ground overlooking Boston, American troops had built a fortification on nearby Breed's Hill. Twenty-four hundred British troops, led by General William Howe, stormed Breed's Hill but were repulsed twice with heavy losses. After the third assault, the Americans, who had exhausted their powder, retreated to Bunker Hill, where nearly a quarter of them were killed or wounded.

14. "Apocalypse": Book of Revelation.

15. "quidnuncs": Busybodies; from the Latin *quid nunc* ("What now?").

16. "the least honorable section": The waisters, who, as Melville explains in chapter 3 of *White-Jacket*, were responsible for tending to "the drainage and sewerage below hatches."

Chapter 9

1. "afterguardsman": In the third chapter of his novel *White-Jacket*, Melville offers this description of the afterguard: "Then there is the *After-guard*, stationed on the Quarter-deck; who, under the Quarter-Masters and Quarter-Gunners, attend to the main-sail and spanker, and help haul the main-brace, and other ropes in the stern of the vessel. The duties assigned to the After-Guard's-Men being comparatively light and easy, and but little

seamanship being expected from them, they are composed chiefly of landsmen; the least robust, least hardy, and least sailor-like of the crew."

2. "Dansker": A Dane.

3. "Haden's etching": *The Breaking Up of the Agamemnon*, a famous 1874 etching by Sir Francis Seymour Haden. (1818–1910).

4. "old Merlin": A wizard or prophet. In Arthurian legend, Merlin was the celebrated magician who help to raise King Arthur. He was both revered and feared for his mysterious powers.

5. "Chiron . . . Achilles": In Greek mythology, the wise centaur (part man, part horse) who tutored the young warrior Achilles. Dipped in the River Styx by his mother, the Nereid Thetis, Achilles was rendered invulnerable to pain or death, except at the heel where she held him. Achilles fought heroically in the Trojan War but was killed by the a poisoned arrow from the bow of the Trojan prince Paris. Thus the phrase "Achilles heel" denotes a point of vulnerability. The comparison of the Dansker to Chiron suggests that we should think of Billy as an Achilles figure.

Chapter 10

1. "rattan": Cane.

2. "with counterfeited glee": In Oliver Goldsmith's poem "The Deserted Village" (1770), the students laugh "with counterfeited glee" at the jokes of their harsh schoolmaster.

Chapter 11

1. "Radcliffean romance": Ann Radcliffe (1764–1823), popular British Gothic novelist best known for *The Mysteries of Udolpho* (1794).

2. "Jonah's toss": Jonah 1:15.

3. "an honest scholar": Melville himself.

4. "Coke and Blackstone": Sir Edward Coke (1552–1634) and Sir William Blackstone (1723–1780), important figures in the development of English law. The famous

Commentaries that bear Blackstone's name were fundamental to the study of English law in Melville's time.

5. "Natural Depravity": A phrase Melville borrowed from the Bohn edition of Plato's works (6 volumes; 1854). It suggests a wickedness that cannot be explained through any appeal to environmental influences.

6. "Calvinism": John Calvin (1509–1564) was a French theologian who founded his doctrine on a belief in "the total depravity of man" as a result of the Fall. Based on Calvin's treatise *The Institutes of the Christian Religion* (1534), Calvinism taught the doctrine of predestination, the idea that human beings are from birth predestined by God for salvation or damnation. The "elect," or "saints," would go to heaven, and the others to hell, without regard to their deeds or their manner of life: God's grace could not be earned. The leading of a good life, however, was taken to be evidence that one belonged to the "elect." Melville distinguishes the Platonic conception of "natural depravity" from Calvin's "total depravity," which applies not simply to individuals but to the entire human race. Melville is suggesting that Claggart's nature is exceptional rather than typical.

7. "mystery of iniquity": "For the mystery of iniquity doth already work: only he who now letteth will let, until he be taken out of the way" (2 Thessalonians 2:7). In this epistle, Paul is beseeching the Thessalonians not to fear the Second Coming of Christ, which could not take place until the Antichrist appeared. *Let* here means "restrain."

Chapter 12

1. "Chang and Eng": Famous Siamese twins who were exhibited in the United States by P. T. Barnum. Melville is likely to have seen them during their visit to Pittsfield, Massachusetts, in August 1853.

2. "that streak of apprehensive jealousy . . . young David": 1 Samuel 16:18, 18:9. Saul was anointed the first king of Israel. David was a shepherd boy who became Saul's armor bearer. David fought Goliath, the giant of the Philistines, and killed him using his slingshot. David and

Jonathan, Saul's son, made a covenant of devoted friendship, but Saul became increasingly envious of David's growing popularity among the Israelites. Twice, Saul sought to kill David with his spear; David nevertheless became a captain in Saul's army and married Saul's daughter Michal. At last, however, David chose to flee from Saul's displeasure. Saul eventually killed himself with his sword after being defeated by the Philistines in a battle in which Jonathan was also slain. David was then anointed king of Judah.

Chapter 13

1. "groundlings": Spectators standing in the pit, the cheapest part of a theater.

2. "scriptural devils": James 2:19.

3. "Pharisee": In the Bible, the name Pharisee means "separated" or "separatist," but it has come to be almost synonymous with "hypocrite," largely because of Christ's address to the Pharisees: "Woe unto you, scribes and Pharisees, hypocrites! because you are like whited sepulchres, which outwardly appear to men beautiful, but are within full of dead men's bones and of all uncleanness" (Matthew 23:27). Christ also related the parable of the Pharisee and the Publican (Luke 18:9–14), in which the humble Publican was praised in opposition to the proud Pharisee, who thanked God that he was better than other men.

4. "Guy Fawkes": Terrorist; Fawkes was a Catholic who conspired to blow up the Houses of Parliament in 1605.

Chapter 14

1. "lee": Sheltered, away from the wind.

2. "the great deadeyes and multiple columned lanyards of the shrouds and backstays": Deadeyes are wooden blocks with holes through which ropes are run. Lanyards are short ropes passed through the deadeyes and used to extend shrouds or stays. Shrouds are ropes that give lateral support to the mast. Backstays help support the masts by

extending from the mastheads to the sides of the ship, slanting a little toward the rear (aft).

3. "Nonconformist": Protestant dissenter, who opposed the religious practices and policies of the Anglican Church.

4. "oratory": Prayer room.

Chapter 15

1. "guineas": Gold coins worth a little more than £1.

2. "Delphic": Oracular.

Chapter 17

1. "Hyperion": In Greek mythology, a Titan, later identified with Apollo, god of manly beauty.

2. "the man of sorrows": Isaiah 53:3, generally thought to be a figure foreshadowing Christ.

3. "the glittering dental satire of a Guise": A French ducal family known for its anti-Protestant activities. The most notorious of the Guises in Protestant eyes was Henri de Guise (1550–1588), who played an active role in the massacre of Huguenots that began on St. Bartholomew's Day (August 24) in 1572. Compare Shakespeare's *Hamlet* (I.v.108): "That one may smile, and smile, and be a villain!"

4. "thews": Muscles.

Chapter 18

1. "up the Straits": The Strait of Gibraltar near Cadiz.

2. "bandsman": Hoist operator.

3. *"genus homo"*: Human race.

4. "mizzentop": The watch assigned to the aftmost mast.

5. "yardarm-end": Used for hangings.

6. "the spokesman . . . Joseph": Jealous of Joseph because he was their father's favorite, Joseph's brothers sold him into slavery, then dipped his coat into the blood of a kid to convince Jacob that his son had been killed by a wild beast (Genesis 37:1–36).

Chapter 19

1. "torpedo fish": The electric ray, whose tail can shock its victim into paralysis.

2. "suffocation": The priestesses of the Roman goddess of the hearth, Vesta, were required to be virgins ("vestal virgins"). Those who were found to be unchaste were killed by suffocation.

3. "the divine judgment on Ananias": Accused by the apostle Peter of lying "unto God," Ananias "fell down, and gave up the ghost" (Acts 5:3–5).

4. "Yet the angel must hang!": Note that Vere is already convinced that Billy must be executed, even before he has convened his court of officers to hear evidence, render a verdict, and recommend a sentence.

5. "drumhead court": An emergency, impromptu military trial; its name is derived from the custom of using a drum as a table in such circumstances.

6. "captain of marines": Captain of the soldiers stationed aboard ship. Sailors and marines generally did not get along well, the sailors believing the marines to be incompetent in matters of the sea. In *White-Jacket,* chapter 89, Melville notes that officers would often play the two groups against each other to maintain discipline in their respective ranks.

Chapter 21

1. "Peter the Barbarian": Peter the Great, (1672–1725), czar of Russia who founded St. Petersburg in 1703 and made it the new Russian capital.

2. "sailing master": Officer charged with navigating the ship.

3. "ship's beam": The widest point of the ship.

4. "short carronades": Light iron cannons (made first in Carron, Scotland).

5. "the ship's weather side . . . the lee side": Vere is standing on the side of the ship from which the wind is blowing, causing him to loom higher than his officers, who are on the lee side (away from the wind).

6. "mystery of iniquity": See note 7 to chapter 11.

7. "casuists": Those who resolve matters of right and wrong through hairsplitting arguments, particularly those who attempt to use scriptural rules to deduce principles of behavior.

8. "the Articles of War": According to Article XXII (as quoted in John McArthur, *Principles and Practice of Naval and Military Courts Martial,* fourth edition [1813]), "If any officer, mariner, soldier, or other person in the fleet, shall strike any of his superior officers, or draw, or offer to draw, or lilt any weapon against him, being in the execution of his office, on any pretense whatsoever, every such person being convicted of such offense, by the sentence of a court martial, shall suffer death." The statute does not suggest, however, that a captain in Vere's position is empowered to convene a drumhead court to enforce it.

9. "the Last Assizes": Judgment Day.

10. "the Mutiny Act": The British Navy operated not under the Mutiny Act of 1689, which applied only to land forces, but under a distinct act of 1749 derived from earlier naval laws. Whether through mistake or intention, Melville departs from fact here, but he provides his readers with no basis for knowing this.

11. "the U.S. brig-of-war *Somers*": While on a training cruise during peacetime in 1842, three crewmen on the *Somers* (including Philip Spencer, an acting midshipman who was the son of the American secretary of war) were hanged for conspiracy to mutiny by Captain Alexander Slidell Mackenzie. The prisoners did not have the benefit of formal arraignment or trial and were not allowed to confront witnesses or offer a defense. The verdict was reached by Mackenzie himself in consultation with his officers, who included Melville's cousin, Lieutenant Guert Gansevoort. Mackenzie was later formally vindicated, but the incident remained controversial.

12. "a writer whom few know": Melville himself.

Chapter 22

1. "even as Abraham may have caught young Isaac": In Genesis 22:1–18, God makes a covenant with the patri-

arch Abraham in which Abraham was to be the father of a multitude of nations. To test Abraham's obedience to him, God tells Abraham to sacrifice the life of his only son, Isaac. Abraham prepares to do as God has commanded, but at the last moment God sends an angel to save the boy.

Chapter 23

1. "wardroom officers": Commissioned officers above the rank of ensign.

Chapter 24

1. "long rammers and shorter linstocks": Rammers are rods for ramming home the charge of a gun; linstocks are forked staffs used to hold a lighted match when firing a cannon.

2. "gyved": Shackled.

3. "the minister of Christ though receiving his stipend from Mars": The servant of the Prince of Peace being paid by the god of war. Melville had commented at length on this contradiction in chapter 38 of *White-Jacket*. Melville viewed the waging of war as a betrayal of Christian ethics.

4. "the Roman triumph of Germanicus": Germanicus Caesar (15 B.C.–A.D. 19), a Roman general who fought against Germanic tribes and was given a triumphal procession in Rome in A.D. 17.

5. "Pope of that time": Pope Gregory I (540?–604).

6. "Fra Angelico's seraphs": During a trip to Florence in 1857, Melville saw paintings by the Renaissance artist Giovanni da Fiesole (1387–1455), also known as Fra Angelico.

7. "gardens of the Hesperides": In Greek mythology, the Hesperides were three sisters who guarded the golden apples that the goddess Hera had received as a marriage gift. They were assisted by the dragon Ladon. As the last of his twelve labors, Hercules slew the dragon and carried some of the apples. The place where these apples grew was referred to as the garden of the Hesperides; the apples were often used by poets to symbolize immortality.

8. "a Tahitian, say, of Captain Cook's time": Captain Cook first visited Tahiti in 1769.

Chapter 25

1. "dropping his mantle to Elisha": See 2 Kings 2:9–15. The prophet in the chariot is Elijah, who ascends to heaven in a chariot of fire, leaving behind his mantle for the prophet Elisha. Elijah is the prophet who denounces Ahab and Jezebel, and in *Moby-Dick,* Melville includes a character named Elijah, who prophesies the doom of Captain Ahab's ship, the *Pequod.*

2. "vapory fleece . . . mystical vision": See Revelation 1:14.

3. "took the full rose of the dawn": The description evokes Christ's ascension in the early morning as reported in the gospels.

Chapter 26

1. "purser": Paymaster.

2. "euthanasia": Melville is not using the word in the modern sense of a merciful death inflicted by someone else. Instead, he is probably evoking both the Greek sense of "willful sacrifice of one's self for one's country" and the description offered by the German philosopher Arthur Schopenhauer (1788–1860), whose work Melville had read: "an easy death, not ushered in by disease, and free from all pain and struggle."

Chapter 27

1. "Orpheus": In Greek mythology, Orpheus is the son of the muse Calliope and a spellbinding musician who follows his wife, Eurydice, into the underworld. His music so delights the god Hades that Orpheus is permitted to bring Eurydice back to the world of the living, provided that he does not look at her as she follows him. On the verge of reaching the upper world, Orpheus fails to hear her and looks back, and Eurydice returns to Hades. Inconsolable, Orpheus refuses to have anything to do with

other women, and he is torn to pieces in a bacchanalian revel by the women of Thrace. The fragments of his body were collected by the Muses and buried at the foot of Mt. Olympus; his head was carried to sea and came ashore at the island of Lesbos, where it became a famous oracle.

Chapter 28

1. "architectural finial": Ornament that forms the top of a column, post, or pillar.
2. "that magical drug": Probably opium.

Chapter 29

1. "an account of the affair": Melville's creation, intended to demonstrate the difference between the "inside" narratives like the one we have just read and the official stories that appear in "authorized" publications.

Chapter 30

1. "BILLY IN THE DARBIES": *Darbies* is an archaic term for chains or handcuffs. This is a revised version of a poem that Melville wrote, together with an accompanying prose headnote, in or around 1886. It became the starting point for the novella.

Critical Excerpts

1. With the mere fact of [Melville's] long silence in our
minds we could not help regarding *Billy Budd* as the last
will and spiritual testament of a man of genius. We could
not help expecting this, if we have any imaginative understanding. Of course, if we are content to dismiss in our
minds, if not in our words, the man of genius as mad,
there is no need to trouble. Some is sure to have told us
that *Billy Budd,* like *Pierre,* is a tissue of naivety and
extravagance: that will be enough. And, truly, *Billy Budd is*
like *Pierre*—startlingly like. Once more Melville is telling
the story of the inevitable and utter disaster of the good
and trying to convey to us that this must be and ought to
be so. . . . He is trying, as it were with his final breath, to
reveal the knowledge that has been haunting him—that
these things must be so and not otherwise. . . .

[*Billy Budd* is] told with a strange combination of naïve
and majestic serenity—the revelation of a mystery. It was
Melville's final word, worthy of him, indisputably a passing beyond the nihilism of *Moby-Dick* to what may seem
to some simple and childish, but will be to others wonder-
ful and divine. (John Middleton Murray, "Herman Melville's Silence," in *Times Literary Supplement,* no. 1173,
1924)

2. If it seems fantastic to compare *Moby-Dick* with
Milton's *Paradise Lost* and assert a parallel conception in
each, it will seem fantastic to say that in a shorter story,
Billy Budd, may be found another *Paradise Regained.* . . .

Exaltation of spirit redeems [the execution scene] from
burdens which otherwise might appear too painful to be
borne. And beyond this, it is innocence that is vindicated,
more conspicuously in death than it could be in life. . . .

Moby-Dick ends in darkness and desolation, for the challenge of Ahab's pride is rebuked by the physical power and the inhumanness of Nature; but *Billy Budd* ends in a brightness of escape, such as the apostle saw when he exclaimed, "O death, where is thy sting?"

Finished but a few months before the author's death and only lately published, *Billy Budd* shows the imaginative faculty still secure and powerful, after nearly forty years' supineness, and the not less striking security of Melville's inward peace. After what storms and secret spiritual turbulence we do not know, except by hints which it is easy to exaggerate, in his last days he re-enters an Eden-like sweetness and serenity, "with calm of mind, all passion spent," and sets his brief, appealing tragedy for witness that evil is defeat and natural goodness invincible in the affections of man. In this, the simplest of stories, told with but little of the old digressive vexatiousness, and based upon recorded incidents, Herman Melville uttered his last everlasting yea, and died before a soul had been allowed to hear him. (John Freeman, *Herman Melville*, Macmillan, 1926)

3. In *Pierre*, Melville had hurled himself into a fury of vituperation against the world; with *Billy Budd* he would justify the ways of God to man. Among the many parallels of contrast between these two books, each is a tragedy (as was Melville's life), but in opposed senses of the term. For tragedy may be viewed not as being essentially the representation of human misery, but rather as the representation of human goodness or nobility. All of the supremest art is tragic: but the tragedy is, in Aristotle's phrase, "the representation of Eudaimonia," or the highest kind of happiness. There is, of course, in this type of tragedy, with its essential quality of encouragement and triumph, no flinching of any horror of tragic life, no shirking of the truth by a feeble idealism, none of the compromises of the so-called "happy ending." The powers of evil and horror must be granted their fullest scope; it is only thus we can triumph over them. Even though in the end the tragic hero finds no friends among the living or the dead, no help in

God, only a deluge of calamity everywhere, yet in the very intensity of his affliction he may reveal the splendour undiscoverable in any gentler fate. Here he has reached, not the bottom, but the crowning peak of fortune—something which neither suffering nor misfortune can touch. Only when worldly disaster has worked its utmost can we realize that there remains something in man's soul which is for ever beyond the grasp of the accidents of existence, with power in its own right to make life beautiful. Only through tragedy of this type could Melville affirm his everlasting yea. The final great revelation—or great illusion—of his life, he uttered in *Billy Budd.* (Raymond Weaver, Introduction, *The Shorter Novels of Herman Melville,* Liveright, 1928)

4. *Billy Budd,* [Melville's] final novel, is not a full-bodied story: there is statement, commentary, illustration, just statement, wise commentary, apt illustration: what is lacking is an independent and living creation. . . . The story itself takes place on the sea, but the sea itself is missing, and even the principal characters are not primarily men: they are actors, symbols. The story gains something by this concentration, perhaps: it is stripped for action, and even Melville's deliberate digressions do not halt it. Each of the characters has a Platonic clarity of form. . . .

[Melville suggests that] good and evil exist in the nature of things, each forever itself, each doomed to war with the other. In the working out of human institutions, evil has a place as well as the good: Vere is contemptuous of Claggart, but cannot do without him: he loves Budd as a son and must condemn him to the noose: justice dictates an act abhorrent to his nature, and only his inner magnanimity keeps it from being revolting. These are the fundamental ambiguities of life: so long as evil exists, the agents that intercept it will also be evil, whilst we accept the world's conditions: the universal articles of war on which our civilizations rest. Rascality may be punished; but beauty and innocence will suffer in that process far more. . . . Melville had been harried by these paradoxes in *Pierre.* At last he was reconciled. He accepted the situation as a tragic necessity; and to meet that tragedy bravely was to find peace, the ultimate peace of resignation, even in an incongruous world. (Lewis Mumford, *Herman Melville,* Literary Guild, 1929)

5. Melville reported in *Pierre* how he fished his line into the deep sea of childhood, and there, as surely as any modern psychoanalyst, discovered all the major complexes that have since received baptism at the hands of Freudians. He peered as deep as any into the origins of sensuality, and in conscious understanding he was the equal of any modern psychologist; in poet divination he has the advantage of most. No doubt the stresses of his own inner life demanded this exceptional awareness. In this book of his old age, the images which he chose for the presentation of his final wisdom move between the antinomies of love and hate, of innocence and malice. From behind—from far behind the main pageant of the story— there seem to fall suggestive shadows of primal, sexual simplicities. In so conscious a symbolist as Melville, it would be surprising if there should be no meaning or half-meaning in the spilling of Billy's soup towards the homosexually-disposed Claggart, in the impotence of Billy's speech in the presence of his accuser, in his swift and deadly answer, or the likening of Claggart's limp, dead body to that of a snake.

It is possible that such incidents might be taken as indications of some unresolved problem in the writer himself. This may be, but when we remember how far Melville had got in the process off self-analysis in *Pierre,* . . . it seems likely that this final book, written nearly forty years after *Pierre,* should contain a further, deeper wisdom. And as the philosophy in it has grown from that of rebellion to that of acceptance, as the symbolic figures of unconscious forces have become always more concrete and objective, so we may assume that these hints are intentional, and that Melville was particularly conscious of what he was doing. . . . (E. L. Grant Watson, "Melville's Testament of Acceptance," in *New England Quarterly* 6, 1933)

6. Judging from the dates on the manuscript of [*Billy Budd*], Melville worked on this final story off and on from the fall of 1888 to the spring of 1891; and even then he did not feel that he had attained "symmetry of form." But though many of its pages are still unfinished, it furnishes a comprehensive restatement of the chief themes and symbols with which he had been concerned so long ago. And he had conceived the idea for a purer, more balanced tragedy than he had ever composed before.

He stated explicitly once again that his was a democratic stage, and affirmed the universality of passion in common men as well as in kings. . . . He chose for his hero a young sailor, impressed into the King's service in the latter years of the eighteenth century, shortly after the Great Mutiny at the Nore. By turning to such material Melville made clear that his thought was not bounded by a narrow nationalism, that the important thing was the inherent tragic quality, no matter where or when it was found. . . . (F. O. Matthiessen, *American Renaissance: Art and Expression in the Age of Emerson and Whitman,* Oxford University Press, 1941)

7. At his death Melville left a mass of manuscript prose and verse sufficient to fill nearly three hundred pages in the standard edition of his works. Little of this merits attention from the literary historian. The one exception is *Billy Budd, Foretopman,* the most expertly wrought of all his stories, a tale so satisfying in the way its tragic theme is explored that it takes its place among the really great works of fiction. With good reason *Billy Budd* has been called "Melville's testament of acceptance," for much of its power comes from the fact that here at last he came to terms with the "mystery of iniquity," content to acquiesce in what he could not, as no mortal can, fully resolve. . . .

When *Moby-Dick* and *Pierre* were conceived Melville was incapable of writing tragedy, though both novels have tragic implications. It was otherwise when he came to the writing of *Billy Budd*. In the story each of the central issues of tragedy is resolved, so far as human insight will permit, and all are harmonized in Captain Vere's speech to the doubtful officers who scruple to condemn Billy. Yet it is Melville's own version of tragedy, constructed after years of painful thought, and the chief enterprise of his maturity and old age.

. . . Only Captain Vere is capable of understanding the law which compels [Billy's] suffering. To the perplexed officers of the court he expounds the law under which they live and by which they must act as agents[:] "We fight at command. If our judgments approve the war, that is but coincidence." Here Melville sets up his everlasting rest. He will not obey the first commandment. He cannot upon compulsion love the God who created the moral order in which we live. But to the rest of the decalogue he at last subscribed. (Willard Thorp, "Herman Melville," in *Literary History of the United States,* Robert E. Spiller et al., editors, Macmillan, 1948)

8. Billy is the type of [the] scapegoat hero, by whose sacrifice the sins of his world are taken away: in this case, the world of the H.M.S. [*Bellipotent*] and the British navy, a world threatened by a mutiny which could destroy it. Melville brought to bear upon such a hero and his traditional fate an imagination of mythic capabilities: I mean an imagination able to detect the intersection of divine, supernatural power and human experience; an imagination which could suggest the theology of life without betraying the limits of literature. . . . In the doctrine of *felix culpa,* the Fall was regarded as fortunate not because of its effect upon Adam the sinner but because of its effect upon God the redeemer; and the world was to be transformed thereafter. Melville's achievement was to recover the higher plane of insight, without intruding God on a machine: by making the culprit himself the redeemer.

. . . We expect our tragic heroes to change and to reveal . . . a dimensionally increased understanding of man's ways or of God's ways to man. Billy is as innocent, as guileless, as trusting as *loving,* when he hangs from the yardarm as when he is taken off the *Rights-of-Man.* What seems like failure, in this respect and on Melville's part, is exactly the heart of accomplishment. For the change effected in the story has to do with the *reader,* as representative of the onlooking world: with the perception forced on him of the indestructible and in some sense the absolute value of "the pristine virtues." The perception is aroused by exposing the Christlike nature of innocence and love, which is to raise those qualities to a higher power—to their highest power. Humanly speaking, those qualities are fatal; but they alone can save the world. (R. W. B. Lewis, *The American Adam: Innocence, Tragedy, and Tradition in the Nineteenth Century*, University of Chicago Press, 1955)

9. The mood [of Melville's last novel] is of reminiscence and profundity. There is much reflection . . . on the problems that are raised by the plight of a serious well-meaning individual, Captain Vere, as he faces some of the insoluble dilemmas involved in man's life in society and in history—dilemmas made specially urgent for him because he is in a position of command and responsibility. . . . There is also an implied lesson: that the appropriate virtues, as we contemplate the fate of man in history, are resignation and stoic forbearance; that the appropriate moods are elegy and pathos; and that there is perhaps the glimmering possibility of grace or spiritual rebirth manifesting itself in history.

Billy Budd, as its opening pages strongly insist, is more political than theological or mythic. . . . It dramatizes the conservative idea that society must follow a middle way of expediency and compromise. Society cannot be based on the contrary absolutes of good and evil represented by Billy Budd and his traducer Claggart. If these absolute extremes enter the arena of society, they assume a revolutionary form and so from the point of view of political realism, it is proper that they should destroy each other. But this is hardly a "resolution" of any sort, except perhaps as showing that contradictions are absorbed in history. The Biblical metaphors Melville uses suggest a quasi-Augustinian idea of grace revealed in history. But still the final impression we get from Melville's story is less the mystery of the incarnation than the mystery entailed in the eternal contradiction of good and evil, the kingdom of light and the kingdom of darkness. The political structure of society cannot countenance this extreme polarity.

But this polarity may, nevertheless, be the very substance of the aesthetic imagination, as indeed, in *Billy Budd*, it is. (Richard Chase, *The American Novel and Its Tradition*, Anchor Books, 1957)

10. On the assumption that "the physical make" is in keeping with "the moral nature," a fair exterior is . . . conventionally equated with goodness, and it is assumed that "the Handsome Sailor" will behave handsomely. But Melville instances the birthmark in Hawthorne's tale to indicate the flaw that so pointedly qualifies Billy's perfection: a stammer, a hesitation of speech, a mental articulation which lags behind his muscular reflexes. Toward him the jet-curled Claggart, master-at-arms, feels an antipathy which might have been sympathy, an animus which is clearly attributable to a frustrated homosexual impulse, though it is set forth as an ethical contrast rather than as a psychological motive. When the angelic Billy is traduced by his diabolical foe, he cannot speak; he is unable to comprehend the malevolence that could bear false witness against him. In his bewilderment, he strikes out, and Claggart is struck dead. If this act is not physically improbable, it is morally indefensible; yet Melville lays it down as the condition of his dilemma. Billy has been "a sort of upright barbarian"; he has shown the primitivistic simplicity of "a period prior to Cain's city and citified man," not unlike Melville's South Sea islanders. He is a specimen of mankind, Melville tells us, "who in the nude might have posed for a statue of young Adam before the Fall." If we follow the parallel, we infer that the original sin was to strike back in revenge against dire provocation; hence Billy . . . is a revenger. And the good man, as [Melville's] Pierre learned from *Hamlet*, has no retaliation which will keep his goodness intact; he cannot fight the world's evils without becoming entrammeled in them himself; whether he resists or suffers them, he is overwhelmed. (Harry Levin, *The Power of Blackness: Hawthorne, Poe, Melville*, Knopf, 1958)

11. "What one notices in him," E. M. Forster said of the Melville of *Billy Budd*, "is that his apprehensions are free

from personal worry." His imagination and compassion work immediately, taking fair and full measure of their impressive objects. This cannot be said of all of Melville's work, in much of which . . . all we can clearly see at times are the features of his own discomposure. And given the circumstances of the writing of *Billy Budd*—his career as an author of books thirty years behind him, his life closing down, his own two boys dead and his old energies gone— we might reasonably expect incoherence, failure of control. Instead we find a concentration, and integrity of performance that match the best in his earlier career. The achievement, and the act of mind it speaks for, are indeed extraordinary. The particulars of this story positively invited misconstruction, as they still invite misinterpretation. Straining after dramatic effect or insistence on an allegorical lesson could only have diminished its grave authority. Mere indignation or pity would have left it no more than a parable of injustice, an exercise in resentment. But there is no indignation or outrage in the telling of *Billy Budd*—no quarrel at all, with God or society or law or nature or any agency of human suffering. Rather there is a poise and sureness of judgment (but at no loss of the appetite for explanation); a compassionate objectivity which, claiming no credit for itself keeps its fine temper before the worst appearances most of all a readiness of apprehension possible only to an actual, measurable greatness of mind. That is to say, there is intellectual magnanimity—which Milton proposed in his treatise on Christian doctrine as the greatest of that "first class of special virtues connected with the duty of man towards himself." (Warner Berthoff, *The Example of Melville*, Princeton University Press, 1962)

12. The encounter between [Billy Budd and Claggart] is played out as a passionate *hatred* [and] eventuates in melodrama. Claggart, who hates Billy with a helpless and ambivalent fury, accuses him to the captain of the ship on which they both serve, meanwhile fixing him with a "mesmeric glance"—"like the hungry lurch of a torpedo fish." Billy, falsely accused and unprepared for treachery, cannot speak but swings in exasperation at Claggart,

killing him with a single blow; and over his sinewless body (more like "a dead snake" than a man), the captain can only exclaim, "Struck dead by an angel of God. Yet the angel must die." Not God himself this time but the instrument of God acted to destroy the blasphemer, and that instrument must bear—according to the laws of men—blood guilt and legal blame. The focus has shifted, with the shifting of Melville's concern and the burning out of his own diabolism, from the Faustian villain-hero [of *Moby-Dick*] to the innocent avenger; and with that shift, Melville's art has moved from the realm of the gothic to that of the sentimental. The abhorrence and pity for the "godlike, ungodly man," crucified on his own evil, kept in so desperate a balance in *Moby-Dick,* has reverted again to the imbalance of [Melville's third novel,] *Redburn.* In *Billy Budd,* however, Claggart is not even permitted the Faustian death-speech of defiance and contempt; the only last words allowed are the submissive ones of Billy, "God bless Captain Vere." The Devil, in whose name *Moby-Dick* received its bloody baptism, has been disowned! (Leslie Fiedler, *Love and Death in the American* Novel, rev. ed., Stein and Day, 1966)

13. There is the ambiguous false ending of *Billy Budd,* where Melville does seem to accept the sailor's death, as "the way things are." But the real moral of the fable comes after and transcends the pretended moral of mutiny and martial law. . . . There is the sudden ironical reference to the battle lanterns that hang over Billy's chained, imprisoned and doomed body. . . . There is the description of the ship's chaplain endeavoring vainly to convert Billy's pagan soul. . . .

"A barbarian Billy radically was," Melville affirmed once more at the story's end. And a barbarian, in this sense, Melville remained, without change, without renunciation, without atonement and without compromise, to the end of his own life. Of course, Billy, unlike Melville, listened politely to the formal theological doctrine of his period. . . . [But] just what is the purpose of a chaplain aboard a man-of-war? "Bluntly put, a chaplain is the minister of the Prince of Peace serving in the host of the god of war—Mars. . . . Why then is he there? Because he indirectly subserves the purpose attested by the cannon; because, too, he lends the sanction of the religion of the meek to that which practically is the abrogation of everything but brute force."

Was *that* the end product of the long centuries of man's heartbreaking struggle for social evolution? Well, at least Melville still thought so toward the close of the nineteenth century; and perhaps even more strongly, if more subtly, in *Billy Budd* than in *Moby-Dick*. Nowhere had he changed his earliest, his primary, his deepest convictions as an artist—those radical convictions that made him the great and original American artist that he was. (Maxwell Geismar, Introduction to *Billy Budd*, Washington Square Press, 1966)

14. To read *Billy Budd* is to feel an intense and indelible sense of helplessness and agony. A youthful sailor, loved by his shipmates for his natural goodness, is put to death for the sake of seemingly formalistic, insensate law. In this final work of Melville's, law and society are portrayed in fundamental opposition to natural man. . . .

Billy Budd is an intensely modern novel. It is concerned with the coming of a materialist, commercial civilization, rational and scientific, in which society grows ever more distant from the rich overflowing of human experience. Billy harks back to a more adventurous and youthful America which, with the frontier and the whaleship, was already passing in Melville's lifetime. Billy's type comes from the "time before steamships," the significant words with which the novel opens.

Melville's last book is a pessimistic view of America's destiny. But the novel does not have a conclusion. As Melville himself says, it lacks an "architectural finial." It looks ahead. Just as Billy, in death, transcends the limitations of the ship's world, so the novel, through the medium of art, transcends the world of Melville's day. For us in this day, the novel is a reminder of the indispensable importance of the artistic vision in the structuring of society—an expression of the need for society to accept the natural in man. Law, as a *creation*, of man, needs the imagination and the insight of art so that it is not drawn in such a way as to imprison the human spirit. Law and society need the help of the artist, to the end that we do not forget man's natural humanity, which is embodied, timelessly and unforgettably, in "the fresh young image of the Handsome Sailor." (Charles A. Reich, "The Tragedy of Justice in *Billy Budd,*" in *The Yale Review* 56, 1967)

15. *Billy Budd* arose from the poetry that Melville was working on during his last, retrospective years. The short novel began as one of many poems whose burden was the recollection of friends and times past. Among the many attitudes that can be isolated in the poems, of which "Billy in the Darbies" was one, two major recurrences are sorrow—indeed, a resentment—occasioned by change, and a nostalgic joy in the celebration of the common sailor as a carefree child who gallantly does his duty. The first attitude is central in the psychology of conservatism—an insistence upon the past for the establishment of values by which the present may be guided. It is an insistence upon history, law, and precedent. But the second attitude, nostalgic joy in recalling the carefree sailor, also enters into Melville's political stance. . . .

Melville's attitude toward the past and change was not something that came to him in his last years only, for his Civil War poems return again and again to the themes of law versus anarchy, of order versus rebellion, and of art versus chaos. Even this last theme is one in which art becomes a metaphor for the ordered control of human affairs (Captain Vere's "forms, measured forms"), synonymous with law. The creation of measured forms became for Melville the highest expression of the human spirit in its struggle with the overwhelming, dark forces of an incomprehensible universe both inside and outside man—the unconquerable, double vastness he indicated in *Moby-Dick* and *Pierre.* There was something protoexistentialist about Melville, as about so many preexistentialist writers who wrestled with similar problems. He seemed to see the universe as enormously beyond a single unifying shape, meaning, or purpose at least for the uses of human comprehension. (Milton R. Stern, Introduction to *Billy Budd, Sailor*, Bobbs-Merrill, 1975)

16. The peculiar air of open-endedness that Melville's novels possess is itself a skillful creation, and his art of elastic circumference helps to show how he produces it. His novels seem so open not because he takes the varied world for his subject and then tries to tie it up into a bulging bundle, although this is the illusion he creates; rather it is because he adopts coherently selective fictional forms and then breaks down their boundaries, reaching out to incorporate what they have excluded. Thus at the end of *Billy Budd* he writes:

> The symmetry of form attainable in pure fiction cannot so readily be achieved in a narration essentially having less to do with fable than with fact. Truth uncompromisingly told will always have its ragged edges; hence the conclusion of such a narration is apt to be less finished than an architectural finial.

But the first twenty-seven chapters of *Billy Budd* are themselves the perfection of polished architectural form. What Melville does—and it is characteristic—is to include as an aftermath three disconnected chapters which suggest alternate versions of the story he has just told. By incorporating these chapters he purposely mars his work's formal perfection and unsettles the settled sense it has made; and these "ragged edges," by roughening his form and making its meaning tentative, give his work the appearance of "truth uncompromisingly told." As novelist Melville must systematize, but he avoids the presumption of having made a final sense of experience by undoing his own systematization in such a way as to emphasize its incompleteness. (Richard Brodhead, *Hawthorne, Melville, and the Novel*, The University of Chicago Press, 1973)

17. Despite *Billy Budd*'s lack of dialogue, its refusal to penetrate the consciousness of the characters, the reader is given almost complete information about the situation in

which the story is grounded. We are allowed no interior views, yet this is part of the essential fairness, as well as the remoteness, of the narrative: it is as if Melville can only fathom and bear his own story if presented in an extreme long shot. . . . As in no other of Melville's works, the tale simply proceeds, straightforwardly, chronologically; the reader is given whatever it is necessary to know. . . .

Also, despite its lack of dialogue, or perhaps because of it, Billy Budd is about communication, and the language and actions which can be trusted to accomplish it. . . . In *Billy Budd* genuine communication does occur although—and this is significant—only off-stage. Vere presumably explains Budd's fate and his own motivation to the young sailor in an interview whose "inviolable" privacy and "holy oblivion" Melville honors. We are told, however, that "in view of the character" of Vere and Budd, "each radically sharing in the rarer qualities of our nature," we may conjecture with the author that Vere explained himself to Billy, that Billy fully understood, that Vere embraced Billy with the passion Abraham felt for Isaac before offering him up "in obedience to the exacting behest." Two men have met and spoken. There is no doubt that in *Billy Budd* Melville has taken his final leave of abundance; he does not believe, as he once did, that he should try to have everything; he is no longer taking revenge on a public which helped to make such an attempt impossible. Melville has muted his material to master it. . . . (Ann Douglas, *The Feminization of American Culture,* Knopf, 1977)

18.   In the final analysis, the question is not: what did Melville really think of Captain Vere? but rather: what is at stake in his way of presenting him? What can we learn from him about the act of judging? Melville seems to be presenting us less with an *object* for judgment than with an *example* of judgment. And the very vehemence with which the critics tend to praise or condemn the justice of Vere's decision indicates that it is judging, not murdering, that Melville is asking us to judge.

And yet Vere's judgment *is* an act of murder. Captain

Vere is a reader who kills, not, like Billy, *instead* of speaking, but rather, precisely *by means of* speaking. While Billy kills through verbal impotence, Vere kills through the very potency and sophistication of rhetoric. Judging, in Vere's case, is nothing less than the wielding of the power of life and death through language. . . .

As a political allegory, Melville's *Billy Budd* is thus much more than a study of good and evil, justice and injustice. It is a dramatization of the twisted relations between knowing and doing, speaking and killing, reading and judging, which make political understanding and action so problematic. . . . The legal order, which attempts to submit "brute force" to "forms, measured forms," can only eliminate violence by transforming violence into the final authority. And cognition, which perhaps begins as a power play against the play of power, can only increase, through its own elaboration, the range of what it tries to dominate. The "deadly space" or "difference" that runs through *Billy Budd* is not located *between* knowledge and action, performance and cognition: it is that which, within cognition, functions as an act: it is that which, within action, prevents us from ever knowing whether what we hit coincides with what we understand. (Barbara Johnson, *The Critical Difference: Essays in the Contemporary Rhetoric of Reading*, Johns Hopkins University Press, 1980)

19. Billy Budd remained, in his final conception, a descendant of Jack Chase, and Melville dedicated Billy's story to him. Billy Budd and Jack Chase were natural children, disinherited of their patrimony. Their authority derived not from the aristocrats who illegitimately fathered them, but from their natural regality. Both were identified with "the rights of man." Both replaced the failed legal family on ship with "the happy family" of fraternal love. But Jack Chase was a mature alternative to figures of legal and inherited authority. Billy, "a flower scarcely yet fully released from the bud," was killed before he bloomed. As Melville reconceived *Billy Budd,* he split his adult mutineer into three: innocent youth, depraved accuser, and figure of naval authority. *Billy Budd* re-

sponded to the emergence of the social question in ante-
bellum America when middle-class fears of servile insurrection focused on workers instead of slaves. But as the
tale developed, it shifted away from presenting mutiny
either as consummated fact or as imminent danger. The
version of the story that Melville left at his death did not
simply participate in patrician anxieties over anarchy; it
also analyzed the anxieties it shared. Just as Ahab had
forced himself into *Moby-Dick* and transformed a sea
adventure into a "wicked book," so the more Melville
worked over *Billy Budd,* the more Captain Vere gained in
complexity and dominated the action. The splitting of
Vere from Billy deprived Melville of his safe havens of
nostalgia, with Jack Gentian ashore and Jack Chase at sea.
It reawakened the conflicts that had characterized his
family history and been sources of his art. It reawakened
them, however, in a new context that made reconciliation
possible. . . . *Billy Budd* reunited instinct with authority
not in Ahab's demonic destructiveness but in Vere's loving
surrender to the state. (Michael Rogin, *Subversive Genealogy: The Politics and Art of Herman Melville,* Knopf,
1983)

20. If we use the technique of indirection advocated
throughout the book and apply this definition of madness
to Vere instead of Claggart, we have an almost perfect fit.
Vere's "cool judgement sagacious and sound" to condemn
Billy may be the act of a true madman "of the most
dangerous sort." The most dangerous madness is not the
clinical sort defined by the surgeon as a variance from
normal manner, but the exceptional sort that retains the
appearance of reason and form. Rather than a deviation
from normal usage, madness can be adherence to usage.
Vere's ordered world can as easily serve the irrational as
control it.

Vere's personal madness can be extended to the entire
society that he serves. Arguing for Budd's death, Vere
eloquently reminds the officers that they owe their allegiance to the king, not to nature. But if we remember our
history, we remember who was king at that time, and we
remember that King George was mad. Thus we have [a]

type of upside-down world. . . . Vere owes his allegiance
to a mad king and the irrational forces of war, yet the
experts considered capable of detecting insanity—the
clergy and men of medicine—are under Vere's command.
British rule of law and order serves the very forces of
chaos and irrationality that it claims to wage war against,
a war fought by either impinging on the rights of military
sailors or emptying prisons of law-breachers. War itself
becomes the master, and it is war's progeny, the Mutiny
Act, defended as the product of man's reason through law,
which condemns Billy Budd to death. What makes the
deceit even more complete is that Captain Vere (along
with those readers who support his stand) is probably not
aware of the madness of his position. Furthermore, no
one, not the chaplain, not Billy's fellow sailors, not even
Billy himself, questions this rule by self-interest masquer-
ading as impartiality. (Brook Thomas, *"Billy Budd* and
the Judgment of Silence," in *Bucknell Review* 27, 1983)

21. In *Billy Budd* . . . the child-like Billy is impressed
from the *Rights-of-Man* and introduced to the "ampler
and more knowing world of a great warship," Melville's
image . . . for warring Christendom itself. In setting Claggart against Billy, Melville seems originally to have intended an illustrative tale on the fate of sensuous,
good-natured innocence amid the mantraps of the world.
As Melville sketched in the nature of Claggart, however,
the undertones of Satanic malice became overtones and
the narrative developed into a reenactment of the Christian Fall that raised the theological problem of evil, first
explored by Melville more than forty years before in
Mardi.

. . . In the closing scenes Melville puts politics and
psychology aside and turns to the imagined spectacle of
two men meeting the inevitable with magnanimity and
strength. The Vere who had argued for coolness in the trial
scene is humanized by sorrow and bent by the weight of a
judgment made with full awareness of tragic sacrifice.
Billy's role—to forgive Vere—is greater still, and his
growth becomes visible at the last when, "spiritualized
now through late experiences so poignantly profound," he

becomes, not a symbol of Christ, but an example of humanity's Christlike capacity for self-transcendence. For some readers there is a pathos too terrible to bear in Billy's "God bless Captain Vere," and it is certainly wrong to take the words as Melville's deathbed affirmation. For a moment, nonetheless, the injustices of the human world and the silences of the divine seem suspended in a mood of hushed contemplation, as if Melville . . . were marveling at what victimized human beings were capable of achieving and what he, the writer, was capable of bringing to life. (Robert Milder, "Herman Melville," in *The Columbia Literary History of the United States,* Emory Elliott, editor, Columbia University Press, 1988)

22. [A] crisis of sexual definition . . . provides the structure of *Billy Budd.* There is a *homosexual* in this text—a homosexual person, presented as different in his essential nature from the normal men around him. That person is John Claggart. At the same time, *every* impulse of *every* person in this book that could at all be called desire could be called homosexual desire, being directed by men exclusively toward men. . . .

In the famous passages of *Billy Budd* in which the narrator claims to try to illuminate for the reader's putatively "normal nature" the peculiarly difficult riddle of "the hidden nature of the master-at-arms" Claggart (a riddle on which, after all, the narrator says, "the point of the present story turn[s]"), the answer to the riddle seems to involve not the substitution of semantically more satisfying alternatives to the epithet "hidden" but merely a series of intensifications of it. . . .

What *was*—Melville asks it—the matter with the master-at-arms? If there is a full answer to this question at all then there are two full answers. Briefly these would be, first, that Claggart is depraved because he is, in his desires, a pervert, of a sort that [at the time the novella was written] had names in several taxonomic systems although scarcely yet, in English, the name "homosexual"; or, second, that Claggart is depraved not because of the male-directed nature of his desire, here seen as natural or innocuous, but, rather, because he feels toward his own desires only terror and loathing (call this "phobia"). The relation between the two possible answers—that Claggart is depraved because homosexual, or alternatively depraved because homophobic—is of course an odd problem. Suffice it here to say that either could qualify him for, and certainly neither would disqualify him from, a designation like "homosexual." (Eve Kosofsky Sedgwick, *Epistemology of the Closet,* University of California Press, 1990)

23. "Billy Budd" is the most wholly fictional of Melville's works. It is not drawn at all directly from his experience, nor does it rework specific documents. . . . Although "Billy Budd" is fiction, Melville's rhetoric is antifictional. Subtitled "An Inside Narrative," "Billy Budd" repeated appeals to the documentary expectations of narrative. Readers should understand that this is "no romance," and it must, therefore, lack "the symmetry of form attainable in pure fiction." Using a term not yet in the language when he began his career, Melville defends his procedures as "realism." As an "inside narrative," the work corrects the news account (itself part of the fiction) of the events it recounts. In 1851, Melville had been happy to encounter a newspaper report that confirmed *Moby-Dick* by reporting a whale's sinking a ship, but now he reenacts a fundamental gesture of self-consciously innovative high culture, from William Wordsworth in the preface to *Lyrical Ballads* (1800) to Joseph Conrad in *The Secret Agent* (1907): defining the truth of one's writing by the falsity of newspapers. As "romance" had been in the 1850s, "realism" in the 1880s was the password for literary narrative. . . .

Combined with the complex realism of its historical narrative, "Billy Budd" equally gains power through allegorical simplification. Billy Budd, the natural child of an unknown lord, an illiterate "upright barbarian," is like "Adam." Claggart, the master-at-arms, serves the ship as its corrupt "chief of police"; his eyes exercise "serpent fascination," and he satanically lies in accusing Billy of treason. . . . Captain Vere, a hero in action yet a meditative reader of "unconventional" books, is the "troubled patriarch" who must resolve the situation. . . . (Jonathan Arac, "Narrative Forms," in *The Cambridge History of American Literature: Volume 2, Prose Writing, 1820–1965,* Sacvan Bercovitch and Cyrus R. K. Patell, editors, Cambridge University Press, 1995)

24. [*Billy Budd*] offers Melville's retrospective account of his own professional failure, his inability or refusal even to dissemble the "innocence" that might have quieted critical fears of his lack of "veracity" and the consequent desire, as one hostile reviewer expressed it, to "freeze him into silence." *Billy Budd* shows with relentless specificity what happens when the hypothesized national poet, conceived as a "novice in the complexities of the factitious life," is actually made to perform in the fictitious life. In order to read Melville's final novel as offering his assessment of a cultural ideology so influential in his day as to determine, to a significant degree, the parameters according to which works of literature would be judged as legitimate or illegitimate, representative or misrepresentative of the infant nation, one must look first to the rage that Emerson named as the silent poet's compensation for a life of mandated marginality. The "river of electricity" that Emerson suggested might one day constitute the inarticulate and enraged poet's compensatory *"dream-power"* is realized in *Billy Budd* as a "vocal current electric" initiated by Claggart's lie about Billy and galvanized by Billy's responsive stuttering and fatal blow to Claggart's forehead. . . .

[In contrast to Ishmael, the narrator of *Moby-Dick,*] the narrator of *Billy Budd* . . . survives not to tell the tale but the telling of his tale. . . . Melville's "final word" is both a confession of defeat, an admission that, at best, his tale offers a "truth whereof I do not vouch," and a manifesto proclaiming the creation of a new genre, defiantly asymmetrical, flaunting its "ragged edges" in the name of the "truth uncompromisingly told." The latter truth is the superior truth of literary creation. . . . (Nancy Ruttenburg, *Democratic Personality: Popular Voice and the Trial of American Authorship,* Stanford University Press, 1998)

25. For Melville healing came to mean reconciliation, a rejoining with a lost, ideal reader, such as Hawthorne, . . . a vital reconnection with someone who perfectly understands him. Melville intended his final work, *Billy Budd,* to do this work of healing. . . .

Put simply, *Billy Budd* is Melville's Trafalgar; it is that moment of resurrection—a rejoining with a lost, ideal reader—that follows the long struggle with falling to mold and oblivion. Melville's final work enables him, like Nelson, to achieve the "most magnificent of all victories to be crowned by his own glorious death," and to bring his legacy to life even after death. Melville would also have been struck by Nelson's creation of a "last brief will and testament," which helps to vitalize into being his rightful legacy. Compelled by a "sort of priestly motive," Nelson dresses his final acts and his person in "the jewelled vouchers of his own shining deeds"; similarly moved, Melville dresses his final act, *Billy Budd,* in ways that . . . allow for "his own shining deeds" to be read and understood perfectly by readers "born in the moment immediately ensuing upon [his] giving up the ghost," readers like Hawthorne. Melville's final work, like Nelson's, can be seen as part of a life designed to come to life again after struggle, war, and death. (Kenneth J. Speirs, "The Deadly Space Between: Image of Union and Mediation in the Works of Herman Melville," Doctoral dissertation, New York University, 1998)

Suggestions for Further Reading

Arac, Jonathan. "Narrative Forms." In *The Cambridge History of American Literature: Volume 2, Prose Writing, 1820–1965,* Sacvan Bercovitch and Cyrus R. K. Patell, eds. New York: Cambridge University Press, 1995. 605–777.

Bercovitch, Sacvan. *The American Jeremiad.* Madison, WI: University of Wisconsin Press, 1978.

Berthoff, Warner. *The Example of Melville.* Princeton, NJ: Princeton University Press, 1962.

Brodhead, Richard. *Hawthorne, Melville, and the Novel.* Chicago: University of Chicago Press, 1973.

Chase, Richard. *The American Novel and Its Tradition.* New York: Anchor Books, 1957.

Dimock, Wai-Chee. *Empire for Liberty: Melville and the Poetics of Individualism.* Princeton, NJ: Princeton University Press, 1988.

Douglas, Ann. *The Feminization of American Culture.* New York: Knopf, 1977.

Feidelson, Charles. *Symbolism and American Literature.* Chicago: University of Chicago Press, 1953.

Fiedler, Leslie. *Love and Death in the American Novel,* rev. ed. New York: Stein and Day, 1966.

Johnson, Barbara. *The Critical Difference: Essays in the Contemporary Rhetoric of Reading.* Baltimore: Johns Hopkins University Press, 1980.

———, ed. *Herman Melville: A Collection of Critical Essays.* Englewood Cliffs, NJ: Prentice-Hall, 1994.

Franklin, H. Bruce. "From Empire to Empire: *Billy Budd, Sailor.*" In *Herman Melville: Reassessments,* A. Robert Lee, ed. London: Barnes and Noble, 1984. 199–216.

Levin, Harry. *The Power of Blackness: Hawthorne, Poe, Melville*. New York: Knopf, 1958.

Levine, Robert S. *The Cambridge Companion to Herman Melville*. New York: Cambridge University Press, 1998.

Lewis, R. W. B. *The American Adam: Innocence, Tragedy, and Tradition in the Nineteenth Century*. Chicago: University of Chicago Press, 1955.

Matthiessen, F. O. *American Renaissance: Art and Expression in the Age of Emerson and Whitman*. New York: Oxford University Press, 1941.

Milder, Robert, ed. *Critical Essays on Melville's Billy Budd, Sailor*. Boston: G. K. Hall, 1989.

Miller, Perry. *The Raven and the Whale: The War of Wits and Words in the Era of Poe and Melville*. New York: Harcourt, Brace, and World, 1956.

Rogin, Michael. *Subversive Genealogy: The Politics and Art of Herman Melville*. New York: Knopf, 1983.

Ruttenburg, Nancy. *Democratic Personality: Popular Voice and the Trial of American Authorship*. Stanford: Stanford University Press, 1998.

Sedgwick, Eve Kosofsky. *Epistemology of the Closet*. Berkeley, CA: University of California Press, 1990.